SUZI LEARNS TO LOVE AGAIN

Upon meeting troublesome pupil Tom's father, Cameron, young schoolteacher Suzi feels an immediate attraction. She is determined not to be drawn into a relationship, knowing she would feel unfaithful to her late husband; but the more time Cameron and Suzi spend together, the more they are captivated by each other. Suzi rediscovers deep emotions, though she agrees with Cameron that Tom must come first . . . But how long can Suzi hide her love for Cameron?

PATRICIA KEYSON

SUZI LEARNS TO LOVE AGAIN

Complete and Unabridged

LINFORD
Leicester

First published in Great Britain in 2013

First Linford Edition
published 2015

C46042480/

A catalogue record for this book is available
from the British Library.

ISBN 978–1–4448–2585–5

Published by
F. A. Thorpe (Publishing)
Anstey, Leicestershire

Set by Words & Graphics Ltd.
Anstey, Leicestershire
Printed and bound in Great Britain by
T. J. International Ltd., Padstow, Cornwall

This book is printed on acid-free paper

1

Suzi was excited about the start of the new summer term. She could hear voices in the entrance hall outside her classroom and it wasn't long before Mr Tanner, the headteacher, appeared with a man and a reluctant small boy. The man was listening intently to Mr Tanner, giving Suzi the chance to look him over. It crossed her mind that he could be the sort of man her gran would call a matinée idol. She went to meet them; she had been looking forward to getting to know her new pupil. Suzi understood how difficult it would be for the young boy to join in with his peers as friendships had already been forged among her class. But she felt confident that after the strangeness of a new school had diminished a little, he would be happy and content. And she would do her very best to help him settle in quickly.

'Hello, you must be Tom,' she said bending down to greet the boy.

'Yes, that's right, Mrs Warner, and this is Mr Sanders, Tom's dad.' Mr Tanner made the introductions. Suzi was aware of the stranger's gaze lingering upon her.

When he spoke, he took her by surprise as he said, 'It's a bit like policemen, teachers seem younger every day.' Mr Sanders shook her hand. 'Nice to meet you. Please call me Cameron.' He ruffled Tom's hair.

'Gerroff, Dad.' Tom pulled away, patting his hair back down where his father had untidied it.

'I hope you have the experience to manage this handful.' Cameron's tone was a little challenging although there was a smile on his face.

Suzi wasn't sure what to say. Sometimes she felt as though she didn't have enough experience to deal with everything that was thrown at her even though she'd successfully deflected a couple of difficult episodes during the past months. She nodded weakly. She had been teaching for nearly a year and had started to feel confident about her abilities and relaxed with her class, but Cameron's self-confident manner caused her to feel unsure of herself. But she knew that parents could be tense when their children were in unfamiliar situations.

Cameron continued, 'I was wondering if you could help me out. I've a bit of a problem in that my work doesn't fit in with school hours so I'm hoping to find someone to look after Tom before and after school. I've arranged to be around this week, but after that . . . '

'Dorcas,' Mr Tanner and Suzi said in unison, exchanging a knowing look.

'Cooee, am I being talked about?' An untidy, plump woman appeared clutching a small child by the hand. 'Nice holiday? Wasn't the weather wonderful? Did you have a lot of chocolate eggs? And plenty of rest?' She let go of the child's hand and pulled some straggling hair behind her ear. 'Go and hang your bag up, Olivia, there's a good girl.'

'I certainly had a good holiday, thank you, and I think we're all ready to face whatever this term brings. And we're going to stick to the rules this term so I must remind you the whistle hasn't gone yet, which means you shouldn't be in here,' Mr Tanner told her firmly, although a twinkle in his eye told Suzi that he was only reprimanding her half-heartedly. Everyone was fond of Dorcas.

'Quite right and I won't do it again, but I had to come and find out who this is!' After efficiently ushering her daughter back into the playground, she beamed at Cameron. 'I'm Dorcas, good to meet you.'

Tom's dad grinned at her. 'Good to meet you, too.'

'Dorcas is an experienced childminder, Mr Sanders, so why don't you see if you can make some arrangements. You couldn't wish for a better person to look after your son. I'll leave you to it.' Mr Tanner turned to Tom. 'I'm sure

4

you'll make lots of new friends and be very happy in Mrs Warner's class. We expect the children in our school to be well behaved and work hard. It makes for a good atmosphere.'

'I'd like to sort things out with you, Dorcas, but I'm afraid I've got to go now, bit of a rush as I need to get to work. If I can just take your number we can discuss things later,' said Cameron.

'Asking for my number already.' She grinned up at him, then scrawled her details on a scrap of paper and handed it to him.

'Thanks.' Cameron turned to his son and Dorcas went back outside. 'Now then, Tommy boy, let's have a great big hug.' Cameron bent down and put his arms around him.

'I don't want you to go, Dad. I don't like it here. I want to go back to my old school in Doonston. I want to live with Nana and Granddad . . . and you . . . and Mummy. I want my mummy, I want my m..u..m..m..y.' Tom's bottom lip wobbled and he sounded tearful.

'Come on now. You're a big boy and we did go all through this last night. I explained to you when you're going to see Nana and Granddad next. I know it's not easy with the move and everything, but I do have to go to work you know.' He hugged his son again. 'Right Mrs Warner, over to you. I'm sure you know how to cope with this type of situation.' He peeled Tom's arms from round his legs and hurriedly made his way to the door.

Suzi was thinking him heartless, when she saw him turning and looking at his son with such love and concern that it caught at her heart. She automatically fingered the simple gold ring hanging on a delicate chain round her neck before tucking it back out of sight inside her blouse. Knowing that the busy school day would wipe out unwanted thoughts from her mind, she was impatient to begin the lessons with the children.

The whistle blew in the playground and the teacher on duty sent Suzi's class in. The children put their lunch-boxes in their trays and chatted excitedly, renewing old friendships after the Easter holiday. Dorcas followed the children into the classroom, fussing over them and chatting easily.

'It's good to be back,' sighed Dorcas.

Suzi laughed. 'You're not one of the children, you know. But I understand what you mean. They sort of grow on you, don't they?' She looked round affectionately at the group of young-sters.

'Yes, but sometimes I wonder if I involve myself with them too much. I expect they are fed up with seeing me around. I probably get on their nerves.'

'The children love you, Dorcas,' smiled Suzi. 'You're great with them. If you ever consider being a teaching assistant, I'm sure Mr Tanner would be delighted. Then maybe later on you'd want to train as a teacher. I know you left school as soon as you could, but it's all possible.'

'I adore youngsters,' sighed Dorcas.

'But I'm not sure I'd be able to confine myself to a classroom. Also, I think I talk too much which means I'd probably get a detention.' She chuckled, tossing her titian tinted curls and looking around. 'I'll just have a quick word with the new lad before I go if that's all right.' Without waiting for a reply, she approached Tom. 'Got to go now, Tom, but you tell that dad of yours to give me a ring. Then if he agrees you can come to mine and meet our dog, Bandit. That's my daughter over there. She's called Olivia. I expect she'll tell you anything you're not sure of, just ask.' Dorcas headed for the door. 'Bye kids, see you later.' With a swirl of her skirt and the tinkle of bangles, she was gone.

The morning passed quickly with the children settling into the routine of school quite happily. All except Tom, who wandered around the classroom taking other children's pencils and crayons and snatching up their books when they were trying to concentrate.

8

Suzi told him off several times, but didn't want to overdo it because she realised he'd been unhappy about coming to his new school. She wished she knew a bit more about his background. From the little she'd heard, it sounded quite complicated.

The next time Tom left his chair and wandered around the room, Suzi gently led him to sit next to her by the window. 'I know it's difficult to get used to us all, Tom,' she said, 'but we hope you'll be happy here. Why don't you tell me what you enjoyed doing at your other school.'

At first she thought he wasn't going to answer her, then he said, 'Drawing. I did drawing. Nana put my pictures on the fridge door with a bit of metal. It was magic I think because it just held my piece of paper without falling off. Don't you think that's clever?'

'Yes, I do,' said Suzi. 'I'm glad you like to draw pictures. I do, too.' She watched as a flicker of interest passed over his face transforming his rather sullen features into those of an attentive young boy. Her insight told her that if only she could penetrate his façade, his behaviour would improve. 'Would you like to do a drawing for your dad? This afternoon we have a painting lesson and everyone makes a picture to take home.'

'I might, but I'd probably do it for my mummy,' he said. 'It might make her come and visit me if I said I had a present for her.' His face took on a closed expression and then he tore off around the room as if their conversation had never taken place.

* * *

At lunchtime, as Suzi was settling down in the staff room to eat her sandwich, Mr Tanner put his head round the door. 'Phone call for you, Suzi. You can take it in my office.'

Suzi wasn't used to receiving personal phone calls at work and wondered who it could be. She desperately hoped it wasn't her mum or dad telling her the other one was ill. 'Hello, Suzi Warner here,' she said her heart hammering in her chest.

'Hello, I just wanted to check on my son.'

It was a parent. She breathed a sigh of relief and settled back in Mr Tanner's chair before looking out at the children in the playground. She wondered if one day she would be head of a school. She'd always been ambitious and Matt had encouraged her by telling her she could achieve anything. Matt . . .

'Mrs Warner? Are you there?' came the male voice at the end of the line.

'Sorry, yes, who is it?' Suzi pulled herself out of her daydream and sat up straight in the chair.

'It's Cameron, Cameron Sanders, Tom's dad. I hope you don't mind me interrupting your lunch. I wanted an update on how he's doing.'

Suzi was pleased to have an opportunity of speaking to Tom's father. 'He hasn't cried since you left, but he has been a bit . . . well, a bit difficult. He's unsettled the other children and there's a troubled atmosphere in the class-room.'

'I imagine you can discipline a six year old.' Suzi heard the disapproval in Cameron's voice and once again felt inadequate momentarily before remind-ing herself that she had no reason to feel like that.

Her confidence returned as she replied, 'Yes, of course, but he's finding it hard. I don't want to put him off school completely. I have to draw a fine line. I understand he's unsettled by a number of things, but children don't always react so badly to changing school and moving house. I've tried talking to him to see if I can find out why he's been behaving as he has.'

'You're the expert, I'm sure you know the best way to deal with difficulties in your classroom. I'll be there at three to collect him.'

When Suzi went back to the staff room to finish her lunch she couldn't eat a thing. Cameron Sanders hadn't been at all helpful in coming up with an explanation as to why his son was exhibiting such bad behaviour. Tom's reference to his mother stayed in her mind. She must try and resolve the situation with her new pupil as soon as possible.

*   *   *

The afternoon flew in a whirl of paint, glue and tissue paper. In spite of Tom's antics, which continued to be disruptive, the children were mainly industrious and enthusiastic. Suzi hardly had time to wash her hands before the final bell of the day rang through the school building. Dorcas bustled in wanting a chat with Suzi while the children packed their spelling words and reading books into their bags in the cloakroom.

'Isn't he a dreamboat?' said Dorcas.

'Who? Are you referring to that gorgeous husband of yours, Fred?' asked Suzi, surprised.

Dorcas giggled.

Then Suzi remembered Cameron who had been out of her mind since their phone call at lunchtime. She'd been far too busy to give him a moment's thought.

'Go on, surely you fancy Cameron, too. He's been on *my* mind all day.'

Suzi smiled, 'Yes, I suppose he is rather good-looking. That golden hair of his is quite attractive,' she admitted.

'How old would you say he is?' persisted Dorcas.

Drawn in now, Suzi perched on a table, 'The bad-boy hairstyle makes him look younger than he is, I reckon. About thirty-five?'

'And his chest,' breathed Dorcas. 'I wonder how far down that tan goes.'

Suzi giggled. 'I thought Mr Tanner would tell him to button his shirt up.'

'Hello, Cameron,' waved Dorcas, spotting him at the classroom door.

Suzi felt embarrassed that they'd been caught talking about him although she was sure he wouldn't have heard

14

any of their conversation. She pulled herself together, directing the children out to their respective parents. 'You should be waiting outside,' she told Cameron, blushing furiously.

'What's Dorcas doing here, then?'

'Me? Oh, I get away with anything.' She took Olivia's hand and they made their exit, Dorcas pausing to give Suzi a wink.

At close quarters again with Cameron, Suzi was amazed at the extraordinary effect he had on her. There was no time to analyse it though, as Tom rushed out from the cloakroom into his dad's arms. 'I hate it here, Dad. They're not nice. It's rubbish and I didn't learn anything new. I want to go back to Scotland. I liked my teacher at the other school, not her.' He glared at Suzi.

She was dismayed by the look of hatred on the little boy's face. Whatever had happened through the day surely it couldn't have provoked such animosity. Sensibly Cameron focused on the paper Tom was holding. 'It looks as though you've been busy. What's that you've got?'

'It's a stupid picture. *She* made me do it.' He tore the picture in half and threw it on the floor. 'I'm not coming back here ever again. I want Mummy.' This time there were no tears threatening, only anger and it was directed at her.

Tom's dad knelt down and collected up the pieces. He looked bashful as he handed them to Suzi. 'Sorry. I see you've got your work cut out. I hadn't realised how strongly he was feeling. I'll have another chat with him tonight. See what I can do.'

As Suzi watched them leave she felt sorry for both father and son and wondered if together they could overcome the difficulties that had upset Tom.

★ ★ ★

Suzi returned to her lodgings after school with both Tom and his father on

16

her mind. Driving along the avenue looking for a parking place, Suzi admitted to herself that she wasn't perhaps quite as good a teacher as she wanted to be. She'd always demanded a lot of herself and wanted to do the best she possibly could. It worried her that Tom hadn't settled a little bit by the end of the day. She held onto the small glimpse she'd had of Tom when he was talking about his nana and wanting his mummy. There was something going on which she didn't understand.

Once in her room she put the kettle on, kicked off her shoes and sank into a chair by the window. She fingered her rings, thinking of her husband. Then she felt for the ring on the chain round her neck. She always wore it except at night when she had it close on the bedside table. Somehow it reassured her. A feeling of guilt overwhelmed her as she drifted into a daydream about Cameron. He was whispering to her and stroking her hair telling her everything would be all right. Abruptly, she started, got up and made a mug of strong tea. Having gulped it down, she splashed her face with cold water and brushed her long, fair hair with deft strokes. Then she settled down with her school work preparation for the following day. She became engrossed in what she was doing and by the time she had a folder full of notes for the day ahead, Cameron had left her mind, but only for a short while as he returned when she set aside her work and contemplated the rest of the evening. Trying to be positive, she hoped that Cameron and Tom would have sorted out what was troubling the child and everything would be all right by tomorrow, but she knew it wouldn't be that easy.

* * *

Suzi drove to school in a buoyant mood singing along with the radio and was pleased that her decision to leave even earlier than usual that morning meant that the traffic was minimal.

She'd never imagined herself living in London; she must visit the various art galleries, museums and exhibitions and not keep disappearing to stay with her parents during the holidays and at weekends. Being a person who firmly believed in making lists, she promised herself that she'd do just that when she got in from work that afternoon. 'Things I want to do and places I want to see' would be a good heading. She warmed to the theme now and mentally added art galleries, museums and street markets to the list. Some time just for herself. She hadn't indulged in that for a long while and it would do her good.

In the classroom, she pinned up the pictures selected from the pile she'd taken home with her the previous evening. She wished she could have put up the one Tom had drawn of his dad. It would have been nice to have Cameron's image on the wall facing her desk. But perhaps that would have been a little too close for comfort. She chuckled when she looked at the pictures the other children had drawn of their families. She remembered Tom's depiction of his dad being a very tall thin man with a large head. And a very big smile.

There was some time to spare before the children were due in the classroom and she seized a chance of indulging herself. Sketching on a sheet of paper on her desk, Suzi tried to capture Cameron's likeness. The shape of his face was easy enough to outline. Then she filled in his fine features, starting with the wide green eyes, moving to his broad Romanesque nose. The square jaw was difficult to get just right, but she had no problem remembering the beaming smile on his generous mouth. Eyeing the far from lifelike resemblance, she copied Tom's actions and tore the drawing into pieces. Suzi was so engrossed with her thoughts she didn't hear someone enter the classroom.

'I hope it's all right to come in.'

Cameron's voice took her by surprise. 'It's just that I've an early appointment and I'm late as it is.'

Embarrassed that he'd almost caught her drawing him, she felt her cheeks growing warm. She'd have to be more careful in future. Pulling herself together she looked at him, freshly shaved, hair still damp from his shower. Faint overtones of citrus cologne wafted towards her and she smiled. 'How lovely to see you.' Then she realised that she was staring Cameron in the eye. Flustered, she turned her gaze towards Tom who was giving her a murderous look. 'Mr Tanner likes pupils to wait for the whistle in the playground, but perhaps Tom could give me a hand to put out some books.' Suzi looked at her watch. 'It's nearly time now, anyway.'

Cameron's sea-green eyes shone as he smiled winningly. 'Thank you so much, I don't want to take advantage of you. Just to keep you informed: I've arranged with Dorcas that she'll pick

21

Tom up at the end of the school day. I think you have to know things like that, don't you?'

Suzi was mesmerised with the idea of Cameron taking advantage of her and had to give herself a mental shake in order to maintain her professionalism.

Cameron continued, 'I'm hoping that she'll agree to bring him in to school as well, possibly after the weekend. I don't want to upset Tom's routine more than necessary, but I have my work, you see. Ring me if you need to.' He bent towards Tom, kissed him goodbye, took the little boy's hand and said, 'See you later, Tommy boy.' And then he was gone.

Suzi realised that she hadn't had a chance to ask if he'd resolved anything during the talk he'd promised to have the previous evening. And by lunch-time, Suzi knew she'd have to phone Cameron as the morning hadn't gone well. Tom had refused to sit still and wandered around the classroom dis-tracting the other pupils from their lessons. When Suzi had tried to talk to him he had sat and sulked, refusing to pay attention to her. In the end, she had ignored him as the rest of the class needed her. 'Cameron? Suzi Warner here. Sorry to disturb your busy schedule, but we need to talk about Tom.'

'I'm in a meeting. Can it wait?'

'No.' Suzi was determined not to back down as it had taken courage to phone him at work. She felt a little irritated that he'd expected her to take his call yesterday lunchtime and now he didn't seem keen to take hers.

'Hold on a minute whilst I go into the corridor — okay, what is it?'

'Tom was upset when you left, but I thought I'd defused the situation with a reading book that he seemed to like. However, he tore out some pages, not just from his book, but other children's as well.'

'I can't believe it. He'd never do anything like that. We've brought him up to respect other people's things and books are very precious in our house.'

'I'm not making it up. Why would you think I'd do that? I wanted you to know so that you can talk to him about it this evening. He's an unsettling influence on us all.' Just as his father is on me, thought Suzi.

'I don't understand why he'd do such a thing. It doesn't sound like my Tom at all. Look, I'm being called back into the meeting, I'll have to go. I don't want to lose my job on top of everything else. That would be the final straw. I'll see you in the morning.'

As Suzi put the phone down, she wished they were meeting for a happier reason.

* * *

After a sleepless night, Suzi was in the classroom early feeling anxious and excited at the thought of her meeting with Cameron. She didn't know why he was having such an effect on her. Lying in bed she'd tried to analyse her

24

feelings for him and for Matt. And now his arrival had her in a fluster and all the things she had planned to say went flying out of her head. She couldn't understand what was going on. She felt she was being pulled apart. On the one hand, she liked and was attracted to Cameron, but on the other, how could the love she had for Matt diminish so quickly? Had it diminished though? She didn't know. All she knew was that she had to control her feelings and deal with the problem of a child in her class being very unhappy.

'So, Tom's progress so far? He's a good little reader isn't he?' Cameron fidgeted in the small chair.

'Yes, but as you know it's his behaviour I'm concerned about. I can't really help him with his school work until his attitude is better. He just isn't receptive at the moment. I did try and explain to you yesterday. He's upsetting the other children by spoiling things for them. They've all settled in really well and get along most of the time. We have odd moments when things are difficult, but nothing like this. I do realise that joining us at a different time from the others can be problematic, but we've all tried to include him and he just doesn't respond. He must be feeling a bit unsettled by the change in school, but I wonder if there's some other reason.'

'What sort of reason?'

Suzi hesitated as she wasn't sure how Cameron would react to what she was about to say. 'Something going on at home. Children's behaviour changes on the death of a pet or when parents separate. That type of thing.'

'I see.' Cameron looked thoughtful. 'Well, sorry to disappoint you, but Tom has two parents and we haven't lost a pet. I admit his mother and I are separated, in fact we're in the painful process of a divorce. Painful for Tom that is, but he's had time to get used to that.'

Suzi was sorry for Tom that his parents weren't living together. She thought it could explain his behaviour, but Cameron didn't seem to agree.

'He's been quite mature about the changes we've had to make so I expect it's just the move that's affected him. He's very fond of my parents so leaving them was quite a wrench, but they speak to him frequently on the phone and we'll visit them in the summer. As far as I'm aware his teacher there didn't have any problems with him at all. He was perfectly happy at that school.'

'Tom did mention his mother and the picture he tore up was done with her in mind. He said he hoped he'd be able to give it to her.' As Suzi said this, her thoughts weren't entirely on Tom. They were also on the words Cameron had said about being separated from his wife.

'This conversation isn't getting us very far, is it? It's Tom's schooling we're supposed to be discussing, not our home life. I realise they might impact on each other, but I give Tom all the love and care I can. He's happy at home with me and is a kind and caring boy. I don't like to hear you say he's unruly.'

Suzi's heart sank. She again felt she was falling short as a teacher. Why couldn't she get through to this little boy and make him happy in her class? Maybe it was, after all, something to do with school rather than his home life. She consoled herself with the thought of all the happy children in her class who were also making good progress with their school work. She must be doing something right. She'd have to see what she could do for Tom.

'I was hoping you'd be able to shed some more light on his behaviour. I hope I haven't wasted your time, Cameron.'

'I'll be off then. Let's hope you can handle this.'

Suzi was sorry Cameron had been so unhelpful. Her day didn't go well. Not only did she feel she was failing Tom, she also felt annoyed that Cameron didn't appear to have much faith in her. It was one of those infrequent days when she felt like giving up. On top of everything else she had the upsetting letter in her bag to worry about as well.

2

At the end of the day Dorcas appeared grinning. She was wearing baggy flour stained dungarees over a check shirt and had her hair tied back in bunches. As usual she looked to be wearing more bangles and rings than stocked by Claire's Accessories. 'I've just made the most fantastic carrot cake, with a delicious cream cheese topping. It's full of yummy ingredients including orange and lemon zest, soft brown sugar and grated carrots, of course. It's great because I feel as though I'm eating healthily when I have some, apart from the sugar that is. You must come round and try it.'

Suzi felt she should go back to her studio flat as she had a lot of preparation for the next day, but she enjoyed Dorcas's friendship and it would be good to have a chat. Anyway, it didn't seem as though she had much option. Dorcas was unrelenting when she'd made her mind up about something.

'Come as soon as you're ready. I know how conscientious you are about your work. But what's that expression about all work and no play? Just remember you're a wonderful teacher, the children all love and respect you.'

Suzi smiled gratefully. That was just what she needed to hear.

'I'll go home and get the kettle on. It's time we had a good catch up.'

Suzi had been to Dorcas's several times before and Dorcas had spent time telling Suzi about her childhood in a children's home and her struggle to find happiness which she now appeared to have found in abundance. Suzi had been pleased to listen as she wasn't ready to talk about her own sadness. She hoped that once again she would be able to keep her past life private. It was difficult for her to talk about Matt and their love for each other.

'We'll sit in the garden, shall we? It's a lovely day.' Dorcas inspected Suzi's face. 'You're very pale, you look as if you need some fresh air.'

Suzi settled herself into a deckchair grouped with several others around a table, set out under an old apple tree. Almost immediately Bandit curled up next to her, his paws resting on her feet. She leant her head back and enjoyed the dappled warmth of the late afternoon sun. The children were playing in the den at the bottom of the garden and she could just hear their voices. To her, the garden was a reflection of its owner with lovely rambling roses and fruit trees among the uncut grass.

'Tea up.' Dorcas arranged the pretty mismatched floral mugs and plates on the table. She cut what remained of the cake into slices. 'Go on, try it and tell me what you think.'

There wasn't much conversation as they enjoyed the tea and cake, although Suzi did praise her friend's baking skills. Once they'd finished, Dorcas fixed her gaze on Suzi. 'It's your turn today. I've told you about me and all my childhood troubles, now I want to know about you. You're a bit of a puzzle. You haven't brought your husband to any of the school functions and you never talk about him. I haven't liked to ask as anytime there is a possibility of us getting onto the subject you close up. Is he some high-flying executive always off on his travels? I know you're in a tiny flat. I suppose that's until your husband joins you. It must be very lonely. You can tell me, can't you? What does he do? You know how nosey I am.'

Suzi hesitated. 'He was a fireman. Hardly high flying, but he was very good at his job.'

'Oh, my goodness.' Dorcas inhaled sharply. 'I didn't realise you were separated. Look, I'm really sorry.'

'Yes, we're separated.' She could feel her grief surfacing. 'Matt died.'

'I'm sorry. Me and my big mouth.'

Dorcas flushed. 'If you'd rather not talk about it, I can tell you about when we all ended up in the Grand Union Canal.'

Recognising the diversion tactics Dorcas was using, Suzi said, 'No, Dorcas, it's time I talked about Matt and what happened.'

'If you're sure.'

She wasn't sure, but if she didn't talk about him how was she going to deal with her loss? Somehow she had to face the fact that he was no longer around. 'We met when we were just eleven and went up to secondary school. We did *everything* together. He'd wanted to be a firefighter right from when he was a little boy. He showed me photos of when he was about five. He was wearing a helmet and little jacket and looked so sweet, proud and determined. And he did it, joined the service as soon as he was old enough. He was good at the job, really good. He always wanted to be where the action was. I'd describe him as fearless. There was talk of promotion. He was so happy, living his dream. We planned our future together. I went to uni in our home town so that we could get married and live together. I've always wanted to be a primary school teacher. It was all working out perfectly when tragedy struck.' Suzi couldn't contain her grief. She put her head in her hands and said huskily, 'I thought maybe I was at a point where I'd be able to talk about it.'

'Another time?' Dorcas put her hand on Suzi's arm and gave it a squeeze. 'Now I understand about the ring you wear and are constantly touching. It's his wedding ring, isn't it?'

Suzi nodded and held the ring which always had the effect of comforting her and giving her strength. After a few moments where pictures of Matt flashed into her head, Suzi suddenly remembered something else that had been at the back of her mind and worrying her. She delved into her bag and, along with a tissue, brought out an official looking letter. She said, 'Read this. The owner of the block where my flat is wants to sell the place. He wants us out as soon as possible. We've all got to find somewhere else to live.'

'But you were happy there. Don't tenants have any rights? They can't just throw you out. Never mind, perhaps you can find somewhere nearer school. This neighbourhood's not too bad, you know. There are some quite decent folk live around here. It would be fun if we were neighbours.'

'Oh, Dorcas,' laughed Suzi, 'you always find an optimistic side, don't you.'

'I bet that Cameron's an optimist as well,' said Dorcas, with a sly look.

'Now how did *he* come into the conversation? Really, Dorcas, you should be ashamed of yourself. You a married woman with a child. You seem to be thinking of him rather a lot.'

'You have to admit that he's nice, though.'

'If it gets you to change the subject, then yes, okay, I'll admit that much.'

'I think he's more than nice. He's such a charmer.'

Believing Cameron to be happily married until his revelation in the classroom, Suzi had tried not to think of him in that light. Her dealings with him had been rather formal and all they'd talked about had been Tom. Surprisingly she did find him attractive, especially as she hadn't thought about men for a long time, but she had no idea if he was a charmer or not, if anything he had been quite curt with her. It didn't matter. She wasn't interested in his personality. He was just another dad of one of her pupils. Pushing herself out of the deckchair she said, 'I'll be off now. I've got loads to do. You'll be pleased to know I've been in touch with some letting agencies and have some places to look at this evening and some of the addresses are around this area. You never know we really *might* soon be neighbours.'

'That would be wonderful. I'll keep a

look out for places to rent and ask round too.'

On the drive home, Suzi was very surprised to find herself thinking of Cameron rather than Matt.

⋆   ⋆   ⋆

She felt a mixture of sadness and a nagging anxiety as she contemplated moving house. She'd thought she'd be able to stay where she was, and able to keep herself to herself. She hardly ever saw any of the other tenants which had suited her until recently when she'd felt more like mixing with people. Trying to feel more positive, she sat on a wall, studying her map, waiting for the agent to meet her.

'Hello,' came a familiar voice, 'what are you doing here?'

'Cameron? I could ask you the same,' said Suzi.

'We live just around the corner.' Cameron waved his hand towards a residential street.

'In that case, we might be neighbours soon. The block where I live is being sold. We've got to look for new accommodation; we've been asked to leave. I'm going to look at a few places now. I hope I'll find something nicer than my present one.'

He said, 'You be careful going into strange places with people you don't know. I'd offer to come with you, but I've got to collect Tom.'

It was nice of him to be bothered, but Suzi was aware of the dangers. She smiled, 'Someone from the letting company is meeting me. That's who I'm waiting for.'

'If you let me know where you'll be, I could look in on the way back, just to make sure you're all right.' He sat on the wall next to Suzi. 'It wouldn't be any trouble. Or I could wait with you until you're met.'

'Really, Cameron, I'm a big girl now, I'll be fine. You go and collect Tom.'

'Will you at least take my mobile

phone number? Then I'll leave you in peace.'

As Suzi entered the number into her phone, Cameron stood up, accidentally brushing against her. The sheaf of papers from the agency scattered over the pavement. Cameron darted round picking them up. He handed them to her and smiled into her eyes. 'Take care.'

This was a different Cameron from the one she'd recently spoken to in the classroom and Suzi felt relieved that the hostility she'd sensed in him had gone. She was touched by his concern even though she regarded herself as capable and independent.

The agent met her as agreed and the two women began their search for Suzi's new home.

'This one has potential,' said the agent, unlocking a room at the top of a semi-detached house in a leafy avenue. 'I can't understand why the landlord hasn't redecorated before letting it out again.' Suzi looked around the dingy room and wrinkled her nose. 'There are others,' said the agent, interpreting Suzi's look correctly.

The next one was a beautiful studio apartment on the ground floor of a smart building at the end of a cul-de-sac. 'This is more like it,' enthused Suzi, already seeing herself living there. 'I didn't realise I could afford something like this.'

The agent frowned. 'To be honest, it's over your budget, but I thought you'd like to see it. A lot of people find they can go higher when presented with something they like.'

'I love it, but I can't go above what I said. It's impossible as I've a car to run and bills to pay. I'm a primary school teacher and it's not the highest paid job in the world.' They exchanged smiles and left the building.

After a full evening of viewing potential places to live, Suzi arrived back home tired and depressed.

★   ★   ★

In the morning Suzi tried to concentrate on the day ahead, but was preoccupied about her accommodation. In the end she decided she would have to put all personal thoughts to one side for the time being in order to be at her best for the children.

Dorcas came hurrying into the classroom late, looking flustered which was most unusual. Even when things were going wrong for her Dorcas usually took things in her stride. One of the things Suzi admired about her was her unflappability.

'Are you all right?' Suzi whispered as Dorcas directed Olivia to the cloakroom.

'Not really,' admitted Dorcas, breathing rapidly, 'I feel awful.' She suddenly turned pale and hurried out. Then Suzi saw her in the playground taking deep breaths.

'Come along, children,' said Suzi, clapping her hands for their attention as they stared at Dorcas through the window. 'Who's got something for the 'show and tell' table?' Suzi asked, hoping that the other mum now looking after Dorcas would be able to cope. She kept an eye on Olivia who would be worried about her mum.

The classroom door flew open and Cameron and Tom hurtled through it. 'I'm sorry we're late,' apologised Cameron not quite meeting Suzi's eye.

'Don't worry, just as long as it doesn't become a regular event,' said Suzi. 'Put your bag on your peg, Tom, and come and sit down with the others, please. There's a space next to Olivia.'

'I haven't got a bag,' replied Tom, making faces at the children.

The rest of the class laughed and now their attention was completely diverted away from Suzi.

'Tom, I told you to come and sit down.'

Cameron hurried out of the room and Suzi could see him talking to Dorcas. Whatever was happening?

Suzi eventually regained control of her class and they had reached the end of the morning when things got out of hand.

'Miss, he pinched me,' complained Olivia.

'Who pinched you?' asked Suzi.

'Tom, Miss.'

Suzi couldn't imagine Tom would do such a thing to his new friend, but nor would Olivia make something like that up. 'Is that right, Tom? Did you pinch Olivia?'

Tom said, 'Yes, I did.' Suzi couldn't fault him for his honesty.

Things were certainly taking a downward turn and they didn't improve when the class took sides as to which child was in the wrong. They subsided into silence as the door opened and Cameron entered.

Suzi was hot and bothered and her words came out in a jumble. The bell for the lunchtime play sounded and she was glad to tell the class they could pack their things away and go outside, except for Tom and Olivia.

When the four of them were left

alone, Cameron said, 'Why is Tom being kept in? What's he done?'

'Nothing,' replied Tom.

'Olivia said Tom pinched her and Tom has just admitted that he did,' explained Suzi.

'I don't think Tom would do a thing like that.' Cameron appeared genuinely perplexed. As he ran a despairing hand over his face, Tom lunged at Olivia and pinched her again. This time he had two adult witnesses who stared at him in shock.

'Olivia, would you go into the playground, please? I'll talk to Tom and his father. And Tom, please would you choose a book to look at and sit at that table by the window. And whatever you do don't tear any pages out.'

Cameron looked so dejected that Suzi wanted to put her arms around him and tell him everything would be all right. She also wanted to feel his warmth comforting her. She moved towards him and he looked up suddenly. 'I'm sorry,' he said. 'I really doubted what you said about Tom, but I've been thinking it over and I may have an explanation for his behaviour. Now I've seen my own son acting like that, I feel ashamed.'

'Really, Cameron, there's no need to. Children behave badly for a reason and they soon get over it. I'm sure he's feeling worse than you now that you've seen him being naughty.'

Cameron nodded to a far corner of the classroom and Suzi and he ensconced themselves as best they could.

'I think I have to acknowledge that Tom may be missing a female influence in his life,' Cameron said. 'When I spoke to you before I thought he had accepted the idea that his mum wouldn't be a big part of his life. He and I are very close and I thought that I would be able to make up to him for the absence of his mother.' He paused.

'The trouble is we can never be sure what's going through their heads.'

'No, you're right and Tom's had to

put up with quite a few changes in a short period of time. My wife and I were working abroad and as she had to travel around the States a lot and as we'd agreed our marriage was over, we decided it would be best if I brought Tom to Britain. I wasn't quite sure of the best thing to do so we visited my parents in Scotland for Christmas and then Tom stayed with them while I searched for a house for Tom and me in London, where I'd managed to get a good job transfer.'

'They all sound like good decisions given the circumstances.'

Cameron gave a brief smile. 'I did what I thought was best, that's all. Tom had an idyllic time with his grandparents and I had a feeling they took him fishing and birdwatching rather than making him attend the school every day. I had a word with my parents a short while ago and they more or less bear out what I thought. He's probably missing them terribly, especially as his mother isn't here either. My parents also let it slip that Tom didn't settle into the school there as well as I had thought. They didn't like to worry me about it. That was quite a shock.'

Suzi opened her mouth to reassure him, but Cameron got in first. 'Please let me finish, I feel a bit of a fool having to admit all this. I can't believe I've messed things up so spectacularly. What I would say is that if there is any way I can help Tom to behave properly and be happy I will.'

Tom sidled up to him. 'Sorry, Dad.'

Suzi felt an intruder as she watched father and son embrace. The sun drifting through the windows highlighted the golden tinges of their hair. She felt a lump in her throat and was glad to be given a few seconds reprieve before they broke away from each other.

After she'd sent Tom out to play, Suzi asked, 'What happened this morning? Mr Tanner is lenient about some things, but lateness isn't one of them. Also, I think Tom needs stability, a definite routine and rushing in late isn't going to help him settle in. It means he started the day in the wrong frame of mind.'

'I am truly sorry. I usually reserve Thursdays for staying at home and getting on with my paperwork and agenda setting. I'm an architect and sometimes I can work from home. I'm really engrossed in the project I have at the moment and I thought I could get ahead of myself first thing, but I ran late. It was my own fault, I had some phone calls to make and the clock had a mind of its own. It definitely won't happen again. I'm determined to give Tom the constancy he obviously needs.'

'Did you come back to school to have a word with Tom?'

'I haven't been able to concentrate on my work. I had to come back to see you.'

Suzi's heart hammered as she took in what he was saying. Had he really come back to see her? What a silly thing to think, she admonished herself. 'How can I help?' She smiled at him, inviting him to talk.

Cameron's worried expression cleared. 'I think we've pretty much covered it all now. You're so easy to talk to. I was worried about Tom's behaviour, rightly so seeing what's just happened. It's so out of character. For the first time in his life, I am at a loss as to know how to deal with him effectively. I came back because I wondered if you had any advice.'

What else could he have come back for? It had been silly of her to think that Cameron had anything other on his mind than Tom. To cover her humiliation, she snapped at him, 'Perhaps it's something you should talk over with his mother. She must have some sort of an opinion on what's best for him.' As he frowned and shifted in his chair, she softened her tone. 'I'm sure you'll find the situation easier when Tom gets used to things.'

'He seems to like Dorcas and he's reluctant to leave her house and come home with me which is good because it means he's happy there at least. I just hope it's not too much for her on top of everything else.' Cameron looked so crestfallen and vulnerable that Suzi had to stop herself reaching out to him.

Briskly gaining her self control, she said, 'I think Dorcas can cope, she's a very capable woman.'

'I've no doubt about that. I just meant with her being pregnant. I don't think she's feeling too good at the moment. You saw what she was like this morning. She seems to be having a tough time with this one.'

Pregnant? Suzi hadn't even known. Briefly, she wondered why she hadn't been told. She couldn't help feeling hurt that Dorcas had informed Cameron before her. She'd definitely make a point of talking to Dorcas when she arrived at the end of the school day.

Suzi could understand why Dorcas might confide in him. There was something about Cameron that made you want to share things. He seemed so understanding. She was startled by the effect Cameron was having on her. She shouldn't be having any of these feelings. If he wasn't the father of one of her pupils things might be easier. About to turn away, she felt Cameron's warm hand on her arm. The touch of his flesh made her jump.

'I'm sorry, I didn't mean to startle you,' he said, his eyes upon her.

It took all of Suzi's strength of mind not to fall into his arms. She wanted to feel his body against her, his lips on hers, but that would have to remain an impossible dream. She tried to shake off these unwanted feelings. Cameron was still scrutinising her and his hand now gripped her arm.

'I'm very lucky you're Tom's teacher. I hope we can work together to make him happy. I'm sorry if I haven't seemed quite as helpful as I should have been. But we're a team and must work together to get Tom through this. I think that we can do it.'

Suzi couldn't speak. Her heart was

beating so loudly she thought it must be audible.

One of the older children entered the room after a small knock on the door. Suzi and Cameron sprang apart. 'Please, Mrs Warner, Mr Tanner says he'd like to see you.'

As Suzi smoothed down her hair and licked her dry lips, Cameron slipped out of the room. She quickly made her way to Mr Tanner's office where she found the door wide open.

'Have a seat, Suzi. There's something I want to talk to you about. As you know from your last review I'm very impressed with your teaching ability. What can I do to give you more experience and help you progress in your career?'

Suzi thought for a moment. 'I think I need more experience with different age groups.'

'Good, good, that's exactly what I've been thinking. After the half term break I'm going to move you all round once a week into different classes. It will give you a more diverse CV. I hope that will suit everyone.'

'It sounds like a very good idea. Thank you. I'll do some preparation in the holiday.'

'I also thought you might take charge of the scenery and props for the summer production the older children are doing. The rehearsals are going well, but Melanie and Kate aren't going to have time for anything other than making sure the children are word and song perfect. As art was your main subject at college I think it's time we made more use of your talents.'

'I'd love to do it. Why don't we send a letter out to the parents and see if anyone wants to help?'

'Excellent idea. We need to bring the parents into the community of the school more. Working in partnership, that's what it's all about.'

'I'll go and get a note printed now and it can go out today.'

Emerging from Mr Tanner's office, Suzi took a deep breath. She was flattered and impressed that the head-teacher had remembered her interest in art. He was excellent at bringing out the best in the teachers as well as the pupils. Perhaps these challenges at work would take her thoughts away from Cameron.

★ ★ ★

When Dorcas collected the children that afternoon she sent them out to play on the equipment in the playground.

'Have you got five minutes, Suzi?'

'Of course, take a seat. I've always got five minutes for you. What is it?' she asked, although she had a feeling she knew what Dorcas was about to tell her.

'I thought you ought to know before someone else tells you, I'm pregnant.' Dorcas beamed.

'Are you?' Suzi hoped she sounded genuinely surprised.

'I thought you'd be taken aback. You don't sound a bit shocked.'

Suzi couldn't help but tell the truth. 'Cameron told me this morning.'

'So I was too late after all. I'm ever so sorry, I wanted you to be the first to know here at school. We hadn't told anyone, but then with me being ill this morning everyone soon knew about it. Isn't it great though? Fred's over the moon. I always wanted more than one. I want a house full. I suppose it's something to do with being alone all those years. I just hope I won't feel too bad over the next few months. I'm going to have to carry on with the childminding especially as my inspection was so good.'

'It was brilliant, but only what you deserve. You'll have a waiting list soon.'

'I'll take them so long as their dads are as good looking as Cameron. He's all we talk about at the school gate. The other parents and childminders were teasing me just now saying I only pretended to be ill so he'd look after me. If only they knew how sick I felt.'

'I'm really sorry for you.'

'Thanks. What's the note about that the children were waving around?'

'I'm asking for help to paint the scenery for the summer production. We won't start until after the half-term holiday and you mustn't even think about volunteering.' Suzi was firm.

'No, I won't. I'm helping with the costumes anyway. We've got most of them done with just the more intricate ones to finish off. There are some in a cupboard behind the stage left over from last year as well.' Dorcas attempted a smile, but it wasn't as broad as the ones Suzi was used to seeing on her face. 'I'll see you tomorrow. I'd better get the kids home and give them some tea.' Dorcas called to the children and wandered towards the school gate. Her steps were slower than usual and, as Suzi watched her, she hoped everything would be all right for her. She'd never seen her like this before.

Suzi tidied a few things away in the classroom then set off for home.

Putting her school folders on the table, she filled the kettle and ransacked the biscuit tin, extracting a couple of chocolate digestives which were just what was called for. She couldn't wait to put her feet up with a cup of tea and her library book. A lack of electricity soon put a stop to that idea.

She looked up the landlord's number and gave him a ring. 'Hello, I'm Suzi Warner, a tenant of yours. I thought you ought to know I don't have any electricity. I've checked the fuse box.' There was no reply. 'Hello, hello, are you still there?'

'Perhaps you'll take the hint. You can't live there if you haven't got electricity, can you?'

It took a while for his harsh words to sink in. 'You don't mean this is deliberate? No, you wouldn't do such a thing. Tenants have rights you know.' Suzi couldn't believe she was being subjected to treatment like this. She'd always paid her rent on time and hadn't had any cause for complaint before.

'Look, I don't want to give you trouble, but I do need to sell the property. I've got an offer if the place is empty. We've a family crisis and I've got to sell.'

Suzi ended the call so that she didn't have to hear any more about the landlord's difficulties and start feeling sorry for him. She felt a little tearful at the thought of losing her home sooner than expected, but tried to put the phone call out of her mind and pull herself together a little so that she could think what to do next. With shaking hands, she picked up her mobile again and pressed in Dorcas's number. She didn't like to bother her when she'd looked so fragile earlier in the afternoon, but she sounded a lot better as she answered the phone, promising to send her husband to help Suzi move her belongings to her house where she was welcome to stay. Suzi breathed a sigh of relief and started stacking things together. She couldn't wait to get out now even if it was what the landlord had been hoping for. It didn't feel like home anymore and she was pleased when Fred appeared at her door.

'Now then Suzi, don't let them get to you. You'll be better off out of here.' As Fred surveyed the room Suzi realised for the first time just how awful it was. The furniture was worn and ugly and the whole place needed a fresh coat of paint. 'I'll help you pack your things and we'll soon have you safe with us.' Fred was efficient and between them it wasn't long before they had everything packed and stowed in the cars.

Dorcas greeted Suzi with an enveloping hug. 'Come in, I'll make up the settee later. Now let's give you a nice cup of tea and you can tell me all about it.'

'Where do you want all the stuff?' Fred asked.

'Just find a corner and pile it up.' Dorcas smiled at him as he gazed forlornly round the cluttered room.

Suzi felt uncomfortable. 'I'm sorry to land on you like this especially as you're not feeling too good, Dorcas. I'll find somewhere else as soon as I can, but it isn't easy. The landlord wasn't very sympathetic. He's got his own problems, but I still don't think he should be making us leave. I'd hoped he might be more reasonable when I rang to report the lack of electricity.' Suzi was close to tears.

'What sort of a landlord is he to treat his tenants like that?' Fred asked.

'It's not right at all. You poor love. Don't you worry about me. I'm right as rain now. You should have set that Cameron onto him,' said Dorcas giving her an impish grin.

That brought a smile to Suzi's face and she admitted, 'It crossed my mind to ring him, but how could he help? Anyway, why would I phone him rather than any of the other mums and dads?' Oddly Suzi's first thought had been to get in touch with Cameron and ask him what she should do. After a short reflection she decided that, in the first place, he wouldn't be interested in her domestic problems, and in the second place, she was loath to admit to him that she couldn't cope. 'I hope I won't be too much trouble being here with you.'

'You can stay here as long as you like, can't she Fred?' Dorcas gave Suzi another comforting hug. Fred nodded as he added some more things to the pile. After some tea and cake, Suzi began to feel a bit better.

'I'm really sorry, Dorcas, as if you haven't got enough to do without having a lodger. But I promise you it's only temporary.'

'I love it. The more the merrier. Just think, I'll be able to put my feet up whilst you two scurry round waiting on me. Although it would have been nice if the circumstances had been better. I don't like the idea of that awful landlord being nasty to you. Anyway, let's forget him, you can make yourself useful. An extra pair of hands is always welcome. Why not start by helping me with supper?'

With Fred and Dorcas making her so welcome, Suzi knew she would soon feel very comfortable in this lovely family home with these generous people.

3

Suzi was holding her head slightly to one side as she put pots of crayons on the tables.

'You really should wait outside,' she told Cameron as he sauntered into the classroom. Seeing him made her feel cheerful although she felt a bit foolish with the way she must look.

'I needed to tell you something.'

Her heart missed a beat and she felt self-conscious. Why was this man having such an effect on her?

'I've had another chat with Tom and I'm hoping he'll be a bit more co-operative. But I would like to know of any incidents so that I can talk to him about them.'

'That's good. I'm all for parents being involved and for information to be shared.'

Cameron put his head to one side

and asked, 'Is something the matter? You look slightly lopsided.'

'Just a crick in my neck. I slept on a settee last night. Don't ask. I had to leave my lodgings in a hurry as the electricity had been disconnected. So I'm staying at Dorcas and Fred's until I find somewhere else.'

★ ★ ★

Cameron thought things over. 'I might have the answer although I'm not sure how you'll take the suggestion. It might not be quite proper. This house we've got has separate accommodation on the top floor. When I knew you were flat hunting it did cross my mind to make the offer, but I didn't know what you'd think. We hardly know each other after all and I thought Mr Tanner and Dorcas might not be very happy. They appear to care a lot about you. However, the flat's perfect for a single person and if you're stuck finding somewhere else it might be your best option.'

He paused, giving her the chance to explain her situation. He wondered if she might mention her husband who appeared to be something of a mystery. He couldn't understand why, if everything was all right between the two of them, she was living on her own. All sorts of possibilities had crossed his mind including the thought that he might be working abroad. When she didn't respond, he continued, 'I couldn't risk letting it to a complete stranger, especially as you have to walk through our part of the house to get in and out. It was converted for the son of the previous occupants so that he had a bit more independence. I think Tom and I can safely share a house with you. What do you think?'

Had he really asked this gorgeous woman to share his house? More than anything he hoped that she'd agree to move in with them. He told himself it would create a more stable atmosphere for Tom, but he knew he was thinking of himself. *Even though he hardly knew Suzi, there was something about her that made him feel as though he'd known her forever. Since meeting her, he'd been completely smitten. Long ago he'd come to the conclusion that he didn't love Wynona any more, but maybe he had no right to plunge Suzi into his domestic upheaval. Trying to convince himself that it would be all right, he focused on the fact that the flat was completely separate; they need not intrude upon each other's lives — unless they wanted to, he added to himself.*

★ ★ ★

'It's a very generous offer, but I'm not sure. Umm, can I think about it?'

And that was just what Suzi did. She couldn't stop herself fantasising about occupying the same house as Cameron Sanders. Although their paths need never cross, she secretly hoped they would. She had every faith that he wouldn't interfere unless she asked him to. It would be good to have someone to chat to occasionally. At her studio she'd rarely seen the other tenants and, although initially she'd been pleased with the lack of contact, she'd started to find it quite lonely. Moving in to the flat in Cameron's house could be a very satisfactory arrangement. But would it be a sensible move considering that she was inextricably drawn to him and he was still married?

*   *   *

'What? He asked you to live in his house and you asked if you could think about it?' Dorcas looked astonished.

'It wouldn't be living in his house exactly because the accommodation is completely separate although I'd get to my front door through his part of the house.'

'Most women would leap at the chance of sharing with him. What's wrong with you? Would you really rather live in one of those awful or horribly expensive places you looked at the other evening rather than take the opportunity to be near that dashing hunk?' She tucked into her soufflé mushroom omelette and salad.

Suzi chewed thoughtfully. The idea of a self-contained flat in Cameron's house sounded idyllic, but she could see there were potential problems. Like how to stop herself romanticising over him every time they bumped into each other. 'I don't know if it would be right because he's got a wife and it might be a bit too close for comfort.' She felt a little self-conscious.

Fred sighed and munched silently.

'Sorry about this girl talk, Fred, but I have to admit we all fancy him like mad. Nothing as exciting as this has happened at the school gates since Kathy turned up with that film star. Talking of film stars, he could be one, couldn't he? What sort of part would he have?' Fred groaned as Dorcas contin-ued, 'I've told Suzi all the gossip about him. Isn't it a fantastic offer? The chance to live in a luxuriously comfortable flat instead of a poky place or sleeping on our settee for ever. And don't forget he's separated from his wife. Ooh, just imagine bumping into Cameron in the morning.' Dorcas's face took on a dreamy look. 'You'll have to make sure you always look your best.'

Suzi suddenly remembered that Cameron's wife would probably be coming to spend time with her son. 'What will Tom's mum think about another woman living under the same roof as her son?'

'It's a business arrangement so what can she think? Anyway, she can't tell Cameron what to do if they're divorcing. He's got to lead his life as he wants, not to please her. Go on, say yes.'

Suzi was aware that Dorcas was losing patience with her and that she appeared to be stubborn without due cause, but she didn't want to rush into something she'd regret. 'I need to think about things. I did ask Mr Tanner if he thought it would be all right and he said that if the accommodation is entirely separate he sees no reason why I shouldn't accept. I'll ring Cameron later with my answer.'

'Just think, you'll be able to walk to my house and to school, of course. You won't need the car half as much. Now Fred why don't you do the clearing up? Suzi and I have a conversation to finish.' Fred pottered about seeming relieved to be away from the women. From what Dorcas had said in the past, he always did his fair share and more with the household chores. He was quite a catch, but no less than Dorcas deserved. Dorcas led Suzi into the sitting room, plumped up the cushions and sank onto the settee, patting the place beside her. 'It's time you finished telling me about Matt. I have a feeling you need to talk about him. What happened?'

'It was awful. There was a fire in one

of those high blocks of flats and the sprinkler system failed. They knew there was a family in the flat on the ninth floor where the fire started and Matt's crew went in to rescue them. There were four fire engines and about twenty firefighters at the scene by that time. They went in and brought out two children and the mother, but she was frantic and said her baby was still in the flat. By that time the smoke was thick and black and, in spite of wearing breathing apparatus, they were told not to go back in, but Matt didn't take any notice and ran back to rescue the baby. He managed to get her out and hand her to the ambulance crew, but he collapsed and died at the scene. I knew as soon as his commanding officer appeared at my door that he was dead. It's what we all dread, that knock on the door.'

'He was a brave man, your Matt.'

'Sometimes I've almost hated him for doing what he did and thought how foolish he was, but I wouldn't have expected anything else from him. That was the Matt I loved. All I've got left are my memories, his wedding ring and his award for bravery.'

'I don't know how you've had the strength to go on.'

'What else can I do? And I know Matt would have wanted me to get on with my life and make the most of it.' Suzi wiped her eyes with a tissue. 'So that's why I'm Mrs Warner. But I think it was a mistake using my married name because now everyone sees my rings and hears me being called Mrs and assumes there's a Mr Warner. I should have made a fresh start, stayed as Miss Marshall instead. It would have been neater somehow.'

'I can sort of see what you mean, but isn't it good to be constantly reminded that you married the man you loved?'

'Mmm, you're right in some ways. I do feel proud that I use his name. He was such a lovely person. It's hard being without him.'

'I wish we'd had the chance to meet

him. He sounds like a very special person. You deserved each other.'

Fred peered round the door. 'I've finished the clearing up. Can I come in now?'

'Course you can, love. Shall we see what's on the telly?' She took Suzi's hand and squeezed it.

Suzi felt wrung out after relating the event that took Matt from her, but knew she had to continue to move forward. 'You two carry on.' Suzi went into the kitchen and picked at some leftover cucumber slices, crunching them while she considered her options. Quite why she'd been putting off getting in touch with Cameron, she wasn't sure. It had been a kind and generous offer — no more, no less. As Dorcas had indicated, she'd be a fool not to take it. She took out her mobile phone. 'If the offer's still on, then yes please, I'd like to become your tenant.'

Suzi could almost see Cameron smiling into the phone as he replied, 'Certainly, Mrs Warner, if you'll sign the agreement, I'll look into some references. Shouldn't take more than a month or two.'

Suzi paced the room. This wasn't what she had in mind at all. On the other hand, there was a small boy in the household and his father would have to be careful. Just because she was a schoolteacher didn't mean she had a golden key to everywhere. Then she heard Cameron's voice again and lifted the phone to her ear. 'I'm sorry, what did you say?'

He let out a rumble of laughter which cut across Suzi's thoughts. 'I said that I was only joking and of course you can come here to live. I'll come round and collect you and your belongings this weekend if that would suit you.'

*   *   *

On Saturday morning, Suzi skipped around folding her bedding and assembling her bits and pieces ready for the move. Fred knocked on the door and brought her a cup of tea.

'All packed up and raring to go?' he asked looking around the chaotic room.

'Yes, today's the day you can have your settee back, Fred,' she said as he put the cup on the table. 'You've been an absolute lifesaver and I'll never forget your kindness.' She put her arms around his skinny frame and plonked a kiss on his unshaven cheek. To her surprise he went bright pink. Abruptly she let him go, not wanting to embarrass him further. 'Is Dorcas up yet?'

'She's back and forward to the bathroom, I'm afraid. She wasn't like this with Olivia.'

'Don't worry, Fred. It won't last for ever.'

Fred's worried face broke into a grin. 'It'll be lovely having a brother or sister for Olivia. I just hope you're right and that Dorcas starts to feel better soon. She's not herself at all despite what she pretends.'

'You'll be able to give her even more care and attention once I'm gone.'

'Now look here,' said Fred, his look serious again, 'don't you put up with any nonsense from this chap. I know Dorcas jokes about Cameron, but we don't know much about him. You're welcome back here at any time. Dorcas thinks a lot of you and, having met you, I can see why.'

'That is so sweet, Fred. Thank you.' Suzi sat down and drank her tea pondering what Fred had said. If only Cameron thought the same of her. But what was she thinking? He was in the process of divorcing his wife and his main concern would quite naturally be Tom.

Cameron was as good as his word and arrived to help load Suzi's belongings into both their cars for the short drive to her new home.

'It's kind of you to offer to move my things. If I'd been doing it on my own I don't know how many trips I'd have had to make in my little car.'

'It's surprising how much baggage we collect over time, isn't it?' mused Cameron, picking up a bag of linen from the floor.

Suzi looked up sharply wondering if he was referring to her possessions or something deeper. But his face was unreadable. Yes, they were both carrying emotional baggage which would have to be dealt with.

At last the cars were full and Cameron jangled his keys in front of his son. Tom, having started a game with Bandit, wasn't keen to leave.

'Ohhh, can't I stay just five more minutes? Pleeease, Dad.' He moved near to the dog as if hoping they'd present a united front.

'Now, Tommy boy, remember what I told you. Dorcas doesn't want to have you here during the weekends as well as weekdays. You'll have plenty of time to be with Bandit another day.'

'I don't mind, Cameron,' Dorcas assured him. 'Tom's very happy here with Olivia and Bandit. We'll have some

78

fun. Why don't you let him stay with us while you're helping your new tenant move in?' She half turned to Suzi and gave her an enormous wink.

4

Suzi hummed as she put things away in her new surroundings. The flat was really spacious and modern. She even had her own washing machine, fridge-freezer and full-sized cooker and she didn't have to scurry along the landing to a shared bathroom. She regarded that as a real luxury. Now she was away from it she realised just how miserable her old place had been. She should have made more effort and added some more homely touches. Somehow she hadn't had any enthusiasm to turn it into a proper home. But this place felt different and she was determined to make the most of it.

From time to time Suzi was aware of Cameron moving about in his part of the house which she found reassuring. And there were snatches of music which she enjoyed. It seemed he liked musicals. She smiled as *All That Jazz* drifted upwards.

She couldn't believe her luck. He'd been so kind in even thinking of letting her have this flat. The rent he was asking was rock bottom and he'd moved her things over without a peep of protest. He appeared to be the perfect landlord. She'd cook him and Tom a meal this evening to show that she wasn't taking him for granted.

As Suzi clattered down the stairs, the phone rang. She could hear Cameron's voice and waited until he'd finished.

'Hi,' she said, feeling slightly awkward and that she might be intruding. 'I've nearly got things straight upstairs. I'm so grateful to you and I'd like to cook a meal for you and Tom this evening. Will that be all right?'

'Tom's staying at Dorcas's for the evening. She's going to give him something to eat.'

'Oh.' Suzi didn't like to press the point and invite Cameron on his own, even though it would be nice. An evening with just him. Suzi let her mind roll on for a while: they wouldn't talk about Tom or school or anything other than the two of them. As she became aware of the silence between them, it was broken by Cameron's deep tones. 'Sorry, what did you say?'

'I said that *I'd* like to eat with you, if that's all right.'

She tried to sum him up. His features were inscrutable. Whatever he was thinking, she was overjoyed that they were going to spend some time together. There was no reason why she couldn't enjoy his company without becoming involved. How many times had she told herself that she'd never feel for anyone the way she'd felt about Matt? He'd been everything she'd ever wanted in a man and it would be hard for anyone to come anywhere close. She really must try to quench those rather unexpected feelings she had for Cameron and regard him only as Tom's dad and her landlord.

'Come up at about six. Will that leave

you enough time to collect Tom later?'

'That'll be fine.' Cameron smiled and touched Suzi's trembling hand. 'I'm looking forward to it.'

★   ★   ★

Having finished arranging her belongings to her satisfaction in her new home, Suzi didn't have time for much shopping. She decided on a simple meal of smoked salmon, new potatoes and salad. It was great to have enough room to entertain properly. She unpacked a pillar box red tablecloth; now would be just the occasion to use it, teamed with soft, white serviettes.

'This all looks very nice,' Cameron said as he sat down at the table. 'Shall I open the wine?'

'Yes, let's toast my new home, my lovely new home.' Suzi looked around feeling happy.

'That's exactly what it is, *your* place, so you must invite anyone you like round. I expect Dorcas and Fred will be the first guests on the list.'

'You're right. And then Mum and Dad will want to come and see. Mum will be pleased I'm not in that cramped studio any more, she thought it was dreadful. It's funny how you get used to things.'

'You'll be in the thick of things here, closer to the school and Dorcas.' Cameron smiled. 'I don't know much about the neighbourhood so haven't a clue what goes on. Perhaps we can find out together.'

'And if I can help in any way at all, I will. I could work in the garden or look after Tom if you need to go out.'

'That's very good of you, but I haven't asked you to live here to be a babysitter. You have your own life to live just as Tom and I have ours. We'll try not to intrude too much.'

They both stuck to safe topics of conversation and continued to talk about the local area and even the weather. Suzi was quite happy with that as she would prefer not to discuss anything personal with Cameron, at least not yet.

Suzi hadn't done much entertaining lately and was enjoying it. Although the meal itself was simple, she'd put effort into presenting it attractively and she hoped Cameron was deriving as much pleasure from the evening as she was.

'That was delicious. A schoolteacher and a cook. Have you any other talents hidden away?' smiled Cameron, wiping his mouth on the serviette before throwing it down on his empty plate. 'Will you have another glass of wine?'

'Not for me, thanks. It was good of you to bring it and the glass I had was delicious.'

'It was the least I could do, considering I virtually invited myself up here. I promise I won't make a habit of it.' Cameron poured himself another glassful. 'It's good that I can walk to collect Tom. Your health and happiness,' he said, toasting her.

Suzi cleared away the crockery and brought out a plate of cheese and biscuits returning to the kitchen to make some fresh coffee. When she came back to the living area, Cameron was looking through her music CDs.

'Hope you don't mind,' he said. 'I'm always interested in what other people like to listen to.'

'You and your wife appear to like musicals,' murmured Suzi before wishing her mouth shut and the words snatched back because he'd know she'd been listening to him.

'That's *my* taste, not my wife's.' Cameron suddenly stood up and seemed to fill the room. 'She phoned earlier. Wynona, my soon to be ex-wife.'

Suzi regretted mentioning Wynona as she didn't want to spend her precious time alone with him talking about his wife, but she was too polite to steer the conversation onwards. 'She's still in America? Working hard? She must live a very exciting life.' Unlike me, thought Suzi as she spent a few minutes comparing life in a London school with a globetrotting experience. At least she was luckier than Wynona in that she had this time alone with Cameron and she was determined to make the most of it.

'Oh, Wynona makes sure her life's exciting. She wouldn't be content with it any other way. That's always been part of the problem. She just couldn't fit Tom and me into her busy schedule.' Cameron's forehead creased into a frown. Then he said, 'By the way, you'd better let me have your phone number in case I need to get in touch and you're not here. Is that all right? After all, I gave you mine.' Cameron fished out his mobile phone.

'Are you collecting everyone's number?' teased Suzi. 'You were quick off the mark to take Dorcas's.'

'Oh yes, I've a little black book especially for the purpose. It's getting quite full now,' returned Cameron. 'I hope I've enough room for yours.' The heart melting smile he gave her showed her he was joking.

Cameron put on a CD that Suzi

hadn't heard for a long time. It had been a favourite with Matt — a sizzling jazz number. Suzi was sure Cameron was going to dance with her. To her shame, she couldn't have cared if Wynona were in the room with them; it was obvious to her that Cameron shared her feelings. As she scrambled to her feet, Cameron came close and said, 'Thanks so much for a very pleasant evening. Being with you is very soothing — just what I needed to help me unwind. I must go and fetch Tom now. Goodnight.'

Suzi couldn't believe she'd got so carried away. Coming down to earth, she supposed it was a compliment. If only there was a possibility that she could be more to Cameron than soothing. Irritably she ran hot water into the sink and got on with the washing up.

* * *

Having left the kitchen clean and tidy, Suzi settled on the settee with her diary to see what she had to look forward to. She was shocked to discover that it was the following weekend when it was her parents' milestone wedding anniversary.

Her phone rang; it was Dorcas wanting to know all about the evening. 'Cameron had a roguish smile on his face when he collected Tom. As though he'd enjoyed the evening. So what happened?'

'Nothing happened, Dorcas. We had something to eat, talked about the weather, and played some music and then it was time for him to collect Tom. I've no idea why he had a roguish smile on his face.'

Despite being cross when Cameron had left very abruptly so soon after the meal, Suzi nevertheless managed a smile into the phone as she imagined Cameron's face puckering with a mischievous look. She was sure he would have been the image of Tom when he was a boy.

'Okay, don't get mad at me, Suzi. You know what a nosey parker I am. I just thought maybe you'd got to know each other a bit better, you know, got a bit closer.'

'Sorry to disappoint you, but we didn't.'

After the call ended, Suzi drifted into her own thoughts once more. She wondered what it was like to be married to the same person for thirty years, although she had to admit that her mum and dad were devoted to each other and to her. They hadn't wanted a surprise party or any fuss made, but Suzi had insisted that they invite family and friends and go to a hotel for a nice meal at the very least. When she was last at home, she'd bought a pretty photo frame decorated with pearls and inserted a picture. It was of her parents caught unawares by the camera in a carefree moment. She'd hidden it away in her bedroom cupboard.

It would be good to help her parents celebrate their time together, but it would also bring painful reminders to Suzi which she should suppress in order not to upset them.

Now she was tired and went to bed hoping to feel refreshed by the morning. But sleep didn't come easily. All night she tossed and turned thinking about Matt and Cameron in turn. She had never thought she'd find another man attractive after Matt, but Cameron had ensnared her and she felt she was being unfaithful to Matt, even though there was no way anything could develop between Cameron and her.

Should she be sharing accommodation with a married man she felt so strongly about? She would quite happily have danced with Cameron if he hadn't gone to fetch Tom. Would she have been prepared to kiss him? No, that would have been unthinkable.

* * *

With her emotions in turmoil she made sure she rarely saw Cameron during that week, but on the Friday evening as she was just about to set off to stay with

91

her parents she bumped into him in the hall.

'Going somewhere?' he asked, indicating her overnight bag.

'To see my parents for the weekend.' Suzi knew she sounded waspish, but she had hoped to escape from the house without coming into contact with him.

'So you're not walking out on us then?'

'Why would I?' she asked, knowing there were sensible reasons why she should do just that.

Cameron shrugged. 'I feel I've offended you in some way. It's as though you've been avoiding me since we had the meal together.'

'I've something on my mind. I don't want to talk about it now. Look I must go.' She pushed past him.

'You're not going in that old banger are you? Here are my keys. Take my car. Tom and I won't be using it this weekend.'

'No, it's okay. Mine will be fine.'

* * *

Sitting in the car on the side of the motorway waiting for the breakdown truck Suzi wondered why she'd been so foolish. Rain lashed down, thunder and lightning scared her and she felt wretched. She checked her phone to see if there was a message saying when the mechanic would come. There was just one text from Cameron:

I hope you arrive safely.
Could you let me know? X

His text message left her with a warm glow which stayed with her during the arduous wait for the recovery service to arrive.

When the mechanic eventually turned up, he was very pleasant and helpful and fixed the car quickly and efficiently.

'Thank you, I thought I was destined to stay in the car all night,' smiled Suzi as he wiped his hands on a cloth.

'Next time you're in trouble and have

to call out the breakdown services tell them you're on your own and you'll get priority treatment.'

Suzi was overwhelmed at the kindness she had received from this young man and from Cameron. She continued on her way anxious now to see her mum and dad.

★　★　★

Her mum made a big fuss of her when she finally got home. 'Suzi you're looking thin,' she said, hugging her tightly. 'Are you eating enough? And tell me about this new flat of yours. All you said was that you'd moved.'

Suzi ignored the 'looking thin' bit and then went on to describe her idyllic flat at the top of Cameron's house. 'My landlord's the father of a new pupil in my class, but Mr Tanner said it was all right.'

As Suzi tucked into the chicken casserole and apple pie her mother had prepared, she chatted easily with her parents, glad to be home. 'Are you ready for the celebrations tomorrow?' she asked.

'I've bought a new dress. I'll show you when you've finished eating. And Dad's got a new shirt. I wanted him to have a new suit, but you know what he's like.'

Up in her parents' bedroom, Suzi's mum paraded around in her pretty floral dress. Then she turned serious and said, 'I know this anniversary dinner will bring back memories for you, Suzi, which was why Dad and I didn't want a big thing made of it. Are you all right?'

'Sometimes I am, Mum. I don't feel too good about Matt at the moment.' Suzi desperately needed to talk to someone and plunged on. 'I've met a man I like,' she began, 'but I feel I'm being unfaithful to Matt. Does that sound silly?'

'Not at all, dear. In fact, it's remarkably normal, I would say. Matt isn't here now and you must live your life, not be constantly in his shadow. Who is the man?'

'His name's Cameron and he has a small son.'

'You mean he's married?' gasped her mother.

'He's separated and he's waiting for a divorce to come through. It's his flat I'm living in.' She took her mother's hand. 'I only said I like him, Mum. It's the first time I've felt attracted to someone since Matt's death. I suppose that's a step forward. I've no idea what his feelings for me are, but he's very nice.'

'I'm not sure it's a good idea for you to be living so close when you obviously feel something for him, dear. Now don't look at me like that and don't try to deny it. I'm your mother, remember? You wouldn't have mentioned this man if he didn't mean quite a lot to you. But your dad and I just want you to be happy, Suzi. That's all we've ever wanted.'

Tucked up in bed with a cup of tea

and her old teddy nestling beside her, Suzi felt snug and safe. She thought back over the evening and then remembered Cameron's text. He'd asked her to let him know that she'd arrived. She imagined him sitting up waiting for her to get in touch. Reaching for her phone she quickly sent a brief message saying she'd got home safely.

But once again sleep eluded her. The honest truth that she couldn't escape from was that her feelings for Cameron were beginning to overwhelm her.

★   ★   ★

Her drive back on Sunday evening was a lot easier. The party had been a joyous celebration and her speech had raised a few chuckles. She thought back to the previous evening and how family and friends had reacted to her. Some people had been wary with her, still thinking of her only as the young woman whose husband had died. She couldn't blame people for the sympathetic glances they gave her, but hoped it wouldn't always be the same. In response she'd thrown herself completely into dancing and partying and exhausted herself in the process.

As soon as she put her key in the lock Cameron was at the door.

'Are you all right? You look tired.' He took her bag and placed it on the stairs. 'Cuppa? Something to eat before you go up? I'd like to cook for you. It won't quite match up to your smoked salmon, but I make a mean cheese on toast.'

Suzi couldn't resist spending some time alone with him and was secretly pleased he had been waiting for her return. She allowed herself to be led into his kitchen. As she sipped tea she watched him prepare the snack. Producing a bottle of mayonnaise from the fridge he said, 'This is the secret ingredient. Spread a little all over the cheese and it browns nicely as well as tasting extra special.'

She hadn't realised how hungry she

was until she took the first bite of his speciality. 'It's delicious,' she said realising that he was watching her closely.

'Good, now how about watching a DVD?'

Whilst Suzi could think of nothing nicer than curling up on the settee with Cameron to watch a film, she reminded herself that it was an impossible situation. 'No thanks, I want to get to bed. In spite of Mum cosseting me all weekend, I didn't sleep well.' Turning on the stairs, she saw that she'd disappointed him, so quickly added, 'It was sweet of you to text. Nice to know someone was thinking of me. You were right about the car.' Climbing up to her flat, Suzi felt optimistic, deciding to look to the future now rather than dwelling on the past. Even though she knew Cameron might not be a permanent part of that future.

5

'Bye Dorcas, have a great holiday. I expect I'll see you during the week. And I'll see you later, Tom.' Suzi watched as they left the building to head for home.

Tom turned round and shouted. 'Please don't forget Honey.'

'I won't,' she called. She leant back in her chair and reflected on the past few weeks. At last things were going smoothly both at work and home.

Mr Tanner wandered in. 'Still here? I'm surprised you haven't left already. Everyone else has rushed off. I think we all need a break.'

'I was just thinking how well things are going.' She neatened a pile of books on her desk.

'Good, I'm very glad to hear it. You've had a tough time and deserve something positive to happen. Your new lodgings are working out all right?' Mr Tanner perched on a table.

'Fantastic. Cameron made it quite clear right from the beginning that he wouldn't be using me as a sitter so I've been able to relax and do what I want. It's a really good arrangement.'

'Mmm, I noticed that Tom was still being cared for by Dorcas. So you don't see much of the boy when you're at home?'

'Very occasionally the three of us eat together and sometimes I read him a story at bedtime.' Suzi loved those evenings when Tom was newly bathed and tucked up in bed eagerly awaiting her story telling.

'His behaviour has certainly improved. He's settled in well now. No sign of the troubled child we saw at the start of term. You've done well with him. I think maybe you're a stabilising influence.'

'I should think it's more likely to be Dorcas who's responsible for that. She's marvellous with children.'

'It's probably the two of you

together. Whoever's responsible, the result is just what we wanted. So, where are you off to for the holiday? Anywhere exciting?'

'I'm going to my parents' house this weekend then I've volunteered to mind Tom for one or two days. Cameron didn't want me to spend my week looking after him, but I insisted. It will be nice for me as I haven't made the most of living here in spite of my good intentions so we're going to see some of the London sights together. But first I need to get the hamster cage and all Honey's paraphernalia to the car.'

'I'll give you a hand with that then I'm off to put my feet up if I'm allowed to. Mrs Tanner will probably have a long list of DIY jobs for me.'

★   ★   ★

Suzi stretched then curled back up wishing she could have a lovely long lie-in. It was the first Monday of the half term holiday and she was looking forward to the week ahead. There was a knock at her front door. Dragging herself out of bed she ran her fingers through her hair and pulled on her dressing gown.

Opening the door she found Tom gently holding Honey. 'She wanted to see you. She missed you. Dad said you went to see your mum and dad at the weekend.'

'Yes, that's right. But it's nice to be back home here with you and Honey. Why don't you two come in, I'm gasping for some tea. Would you like some milk?'

'Yes.'

'Please — mind your manners, Tom.' Cameron appeared at the top of the stairs. He looked at Suzi and raised his eyebrows. 'Sorry we're a bit early, but Honey couldn't wait to see you. I was anxious to see you too.'

She felt he was teasing and said nothing.

'I was worried because if you'd

forgotten I'd be in big trouble at work. You didn't forget, did you? That you said you'd have Tom whilst I'm working today.'

'No, just overslept. We're going to have a great time.' Suzi wished she'd set her alarm clock to go off earlier so she could have had a chance to shower and dress before her visitors arrived. She felt awkward facing Cameron in her dressing gown.

'I'm taking tomorrow as leave so you can have the whole day in bed if you like. I'm off then. See you Tom, bye Honey, have fun Mrs Warner.' Cameron winked at her and dashed off down the stairs.

Tom barely glanced up as he continued to stroke the hamster. 'I like you. My dad likes you, too. You make him happy.'

'Do I? How do you know?' Suzi was aching to know the answer.

'Just things he says. Like you're a good cook and he wishes you'd cook for us more often.'

'Right.' Nothing great then. But why should she care? He wasn't interested in her and he was still dealing with the split from his wife. But where was Wynona? Surely she'd want to see her son during the holidays. She'd heard Tom talking to his mum on the phone, but as far as she knew he hadn't seen her since at least the start of the summer term. As she'd been making her way downstairs once, she'd also heard Cameron on the phone talking angrily to Wynona.

Tom interrupted her thoughts. 'I liked that pizza you did when you let me put the toppings on. Will you cook for us again?'

'We'll see, Tom, now why don't you go and put Honey in her cage. Make sure you put the catch on the door. Then come back up and help yourself to a book from your special shelf whilst I get ready. Then we'll set off and explore London for the day. I wonder what we'll see. It's going to be a very exciting and interesting day.'

* * *

Suzi and Tom were both exhausted when they arrived back home late in the afternoon.

'Suzi, can we please watch one of my DVDs? Dad won't mind.'

Curling up together on the settee downstairs they watched *The Lion King* until they couldn't keep their eyes open any longer. They were woken by Cameron clattering in the kitchen.

'Hey, Dad,' Tom called.

Cameron walked into the room and bent to kiss Tom. 'You both looked so peaceful, I didn't like to disturb you. Pasta's nearly ready. Tell me what you did today. From the look of you both it must have been something very tiring.'

'We went on the tube and I read the map. We went to loads of places, Dad. I think we even saw the top of your office from that eye thing. When we were getting on the big wheel a man said, 'Hold your mummy's hand', so I held Suzi's.'

Suzi waited for Cameron's reaction, hoping he wouldn't be offended that she'd been mistaken for Tom's mother.

'That was a good idea. Suzi's hand is a very safe one to hold. If I'd been there I'd have done the same.'

'Don't be silly, Dad,' Tom said, shaking his head. 'That man wouldn't think Suzi was *your* mum! You're too old. You've got wrinkles.'

'Only by my eyes and anyway they're laughter lines not wrinkles.' Cameron put on a look, pretending to be affronted.

Suzi giggled at Cameron and Tom's easy banter.

'I want to call Suzi, Mum Two,' insisted Tom, making his dad laugh.

'You'll have to take that up with Suzi.'

An earnest discussion between Suzi and Tom followed as Cameron popped back into the kitchen.

'You had a good day, then?' continued Cameron, when he returned.

'Yeah. It was great. I want a talking dog.'

'It was a man in a sort of kennel with his head sticking out. His head was made up like a dog's.' Suzi felt an explanation was required. 'He was on the South Bank. We also saw some of those people painted bronze or silver and standing still like statues. They're amazing.'

'Some people were trying to make them laugh,' said Tom, 'but it wasn't fair. I wouldn't like anyone to do that to me if I had to keep still for something. And we saw a woman riding a bike with one wheel.'

'A unicycle? Sounds as though you've had an exciting time. Well, I've got an exciting bit of news, too.' Cameron beamed at his son.

'Mummy's coming?' The way Tom leant forward, his eyes sparkling with expectation tugged at Suzi's heart.

'No, not Mummy, but I'm sure she'll come and see you soon. You know she's very busy at work and it's difficult because she lives in America. You remember how long it takes to get from there to here.' Cameron and Suzi exchanged an understanding look.

Tom didn't look convinced.

'So go on, guess who is coming,' Cameron insisted.

'I don't know.' It didn't sound as though Tom would be pleased whoever it was. His earlier enthusiasm seemed to be knocked out of him by the disappointment of not seeing his mother.

'Nana and Granddad rang me at work this morning and said they're on their way down from Scotland and would like to take you to Brighton for a few days.'

Tom's face lit up again. 'Goody, Nana and Granddad, Nana and Grand-dad.' Tom sang as he danced round the room then stopped suddenly. 'What's Brighton?'

'It's the seaside. Why don't you two do the clearing up when we've finished eating? I'll go and see to the bed in the spare room. They'll be here very late, long after you've gone to bed and they'll be very tired from all that driving.'

Suzi rummaged in her bag. 'You'll need a bucket and spade if you're going to the seaside,' she said, giving Tom some cash.

'Cor, thanks.' Tom grinned and pocketed the money.

* * *

Once all the jobs were done and Tom had packed a few things, Suzi slumped in an armchair. 'I never knew how exhausting children are.'

It was only when Cameron laughed that she realised what a silly thing she'd said.

'But really, a class of children is less exhausting than taking one round London. He's interested in everything and constantly asking questions. It was lovely, but he wore me out.' She yawned.

'You deserve some pampering. *You* need looking after now. How about a glass of wine?'

'Perhaps I should go. I'm not sure . . . '

'As a thank you. Please.'

'All right, but I'm not stopping long.'

They sat in silence as they sipped the sparkling wine.

'I was wondering . . . ' Cameron began then stopped. 'I'm not sure what you'll make of this.'

'You'll never know if you don't say it,' Suzi said giggling although she was slightly worried about what he might be about to propose.

'Well, you wouldn't spend the day with me tomorrow would you? I was looking forward to the Natural History Museum with Tom and now with him going . . . '

'Is it a good idea?' Suzi regretted asking as soon as she'd posed the question. She could think of nothing nicer than spending the day with this striking man. Surely they could treat themselves to a day in town together without it being analysed in too great detail.

'In what way? Depending where we go, it could be educational and you might get some ideas for projects at school. Or do you mean because I'm your landlord?'

'I admit I didn't go out with my previous landlord. I meant because you are married,' said Suzi. She wanted both of them to be clear about the impossibility of a relationship between them.

'Hardly! The divorce should be through any day now, but I don't see how that impacts on a day out together,' replied Cameron, looking puzzled. 'We'd merely be having a day out as landlord and tenant.' Cameron's mock pomposity gave way to a rumble of laughter. Then he became serious as he asked, 'Is there some problem for you? What is it you're concerned about?'

Suzi wanted to tell him about Matt, but she couldn't find the words and suddenly it was too late.

'Come on, Suzi, say you'll come with me and let's drink to a fun day out.'

* * *

When Suzi woke the following morning, rain was beating against her window. A museum or gallery visit seemed a better option than the seaside and she felt sorry for Tom. When she heard his shrieks of laughter coming up the stairs she knew the weather was totally irrelevant to his enjoyment.

Although Suzi would have been pleased to meet Cameron's parents, she didn't want to intrude on a family get together, so she stayed upstairs listening to the sounds of doors slamming and luggage being trundled downstairs. Eventually the front door slammed and the house was quiet. She dressed with care in linen slacks with a smock top and was ready at the agreed time and excited about the day ahead despite the few misgivings she'd had the previous evening. The rain had stopped by that time, but the skies weren't clear so she grabbed a light waterproof jacket. As she walked down the stairs Cameron waited at the bottom and eyed her appreciatively.

'Looking good *and* on time. You could give Wynona a few tips about being punctual.'

The way he said his wife's name puzzled Suzi. There was an element of anger in his voice.

'You're nicer to Tom, too.' He turned abruptly.

The way he spat his remarks about Wynona had Suzi wondering if perhaps the divorce wasn't proving to be easy or amicable, but perhaps they rarely were. She would have liked Cameron and Wynona to at least try to get on for the sake of Tom even though there might be no love left between them.

6

They'd barely spoken on their walk to the underground station and Suzi felt uncomfortable as they sat in silence on the tube train into central London. Things weren't working out as well as she'd hoped. She was quite sure she'd done nothing to upset Cameron. He'd never been in this sort of a mood with her before. It wasn't going to be a pleasant day if his frame of mind didn't change. She would have to see what could be done to cheer him up.

'Tom got off okay then?' she ventured.

'Yes, about nine. He was very excited and Mum and Dad were glad to be with him again. They adore him. I just hope they don't unsettle him. He's been so happy recently, I can't thank you enough. You've helped to give him some stability.' He gave her one of his heart-melting smiles.

'How nice of you to say so,' said Suzi. 'I'm not sure how much I've helped. I expect the fact that you're both settled in the house and have a routine has been good for him. And of course Dorcas has played a big part as well.'

'You're right, she's been marvellous,' acknowledged Cameron. 'She has a wonderful rapport with the children. She makes a perfect mother. It's brilliant watching her and Fred now she's expecting another little one. I remember Tom when he was first born. I've never been so scared of anything in my life.' He let out a snort of laughter. 'I expect you think I'm silly, but love can do all sorts of things to you, it's quite scary the power it has.' Cameron stopped talking for a short while and stared into the distance. Then he studied the underground map and asked, 'Now, where are we going?'

'I thought *you'd* already decided.' Suzi's reply came out more sharply than she'd meant it to, but his remarks about love had unnerved her somewhat.

'Sorry,' Cameron looked a little sheepish. 'I didn't mean to spoil our outing. It's no excuse, but I've got some stuff on my mind and it's made me behave badly. I shouldn't let it mess up our time together. I don't suppose you're interested in my marital problems, why should you be? So let's just say Wynona isn't making life easy. But let's forget all that. What would you like to do today?'

'I did wonder about the National Gallery, but maybe you'd prefer . . . '

'That would be just right. It's one of the places I want to visit. That's Charing Cross, so we don't need to change.'

'I made a list of things I want to do while I'm in London, but I haven't managed many of them yet,' said Suzi.

'Me too,' said Cameron. 'Perhaps we can pool our wish lists and go on more outings together.'

Suzi felt as though she was in a dream. As they crossed Trafalgar

117

Square she glanced at Cameron and felt elated to be with him. She couldn't believe she was spending the day with this stunning man.

Once inside the gallery Cameron said, 'You choose what we see first. I really don't mind at all. It will all be interesting.'

'Let's have a look at the catalogue. The seventeenth century painters might be a good place to start. What do you think?' She held out the page for Cameron to see, but he didn't even glance at it.

'I'm sure it'll be fascinating. Which floor do we need?'

They found the collection and were both immersed in their own thoughts as they toured the room.

As Suzi's tummy gave a small protest that breakfast, such as it had been, was a long time ago, she noticed that Cameron was behaving rather oddly. He was skulking around the edge of the room with his eyes trained on a man seated near the back wall. She wondered if the room attendant would become suspicious. Instead of admiring the Rubens painting, Cameron had eyes only for the man. As she studied them both, Suzi understood what was happening. The man was sketching the oil painting and Cameron wanted to inspect it. Suzi, with a pragmatism which surprised her, walked straight up to the man and asked, 'May I?' Behind her she heard Cameron's gasp of surprise.

The man nodded, but didn't take his gaze off the painting or his attention away from his work. Suzi was interested in art and knew what she liked. She very much liked this copy. Samson and Delilah were brought to life by him, and the contours of the muscles on Samson's back caused her a sharp intake of breath. It was, quite simply, beautiful.

A hand on her arm was pulling her away. 'We shouldn't disturb him when he's so absorbed.'

'I just wanted to see what you were obviously engrossed in.'

Cameron whispered, 'I'd love to do that, you know. Come in here and sketch some of these things.'

'I think you can, you just bring a seat of some sort and a sketch pad, plus your pencils and so on.' Suzi watched as Cameron's eyes lit up. 'I didn't know you liked to draw. I haven't seen any of your work up in the house.'

'I don't have much time at the moment, but before Tom was born, I used to take off into the country and sketch horses in a field, or trees in a wood. Then, suddenly, there was no time. I'm determined to take it up again. Of course my work involves creativity, but of a completely different sort. I like letting my imagination run away with me.'

His enthusiasm was obvious and infectious. It seemed to Suzi that he was more relaxed away from Tom, probably because he didn't have the weight of responsibility. He must be finding caring for his son on his own quite difficult. Suzi said, 'You could come into school and work with Year Five. I know Mr Tanner's always happy to have parental involvement and he'd snap you up as you're so talented.'

'How can you say that?' laughed Cameron, although he looked quite pleased at the compliment. 'You haven't seen any of my work.'

Suzi brushed this aside, carried away on her own tide of eagerness. 'And if any of the children find the actual drawing difficult, we could find things for them to do rubbings of. Oh, it'll be great fun. Please say you'll do it.' Suzi waited, hoping he'd agree. Encouraging him, she added, 'I'm sure we'd work well together, don't you think?'

'It sounds ideal,' agreed Cameron. 'We could spend the evenings preparing, discussing the best media, looking out pictures for them to copy, just like that man over there.'

Suzi's eyes shone as she looked at

Cameron, willing him to say yes.

This time, Cameron put his hands securely on her shoulders and said, 'Let's keep a sense of proportion about this. I haven't time to devote to the school. I'm either at work or looking after Tom. I don't have time for anything else. The children need and deserve somebody they can build up a rapport with, someone they can trust. I just can't promise to put aside a time for them every week.'

Suzi opened her mouth to protest, but as she thought about it she knew that what he'd said was correct. She was surprised and delighted at his intuition. For a short time she'd envisaged him coming to the school and the two of them preparing Year Five for their journey onward and upward into secondary school and now she crashed back to the real world. Suzi wondered if he might be implying he didn't have time for her.

Sitting in the café, having placed her food order with Cameron who was now queuing, Suzi took stock of the situation. She must be realistic she told herself. *She* might be a free agent, but Cameron most definitely was not yet and anyway he'd just made it quite clear that he only had time for work and Tom. There might well be no place in his life for her. Just make the most of today, she told herself firmly.

'You're looking thoughtful.' Cameron unloaded the tray and sat opposite her. 'You are having a good time, aren't you?'

'It's incredible,' breathed Suzi, hoping he couldn't read her mind. 'It's been a fantastic morning. I wish I could do this more often.'

'Pity I can't take more leave, I'd love to continue our visits around the London sights together, but I want to have Friday off for when Tom gets back.'

'Landlords don't usually take holiday to entertain their tenants.' Suzi was struggling to relax with him now.

'I'd like to think you're a bit more

than just my tenant.' He placed his hand on hers.

'But there are a lot of complications in your life like Tom and the fact that you are still married!'

Cameron pulled his hand back as though he'd been scalded. 'So are you, *Mrs* Warner.' He cleared his throat and said softly, 'I thought we were friends. Isn't it possible for a man and woman to just be friends? And I agree that I am technically still married, but that will be over soon. I'm not pretending it's easy, but I think closure will help Tom and me to move on. Of course he will still want to see Wynona, but I'm sure she'll remain living in the States. Anyway, what about you? Do you have anything to tell me about your background? You must have a past.' The words sounded clipped and cut Suzi to the quick.

She was desperate to tell Cameron about Matt, but the crowded atmosphere made it impossible. At least he'd been straightforward with her about his marital situation and, by omission, she hadn't given him the same courtesy. She picked at her salad in silence, feeling confused.

'I'm sorry,' Cameron said, taking her hand again. 'As I said I've got a few things on my mind, mostly to do with Tom, but I shouldn't take it out on you. I didn't mean to sound grumpy.' He ran his fingers through his hair and looked dejected.

Immediately Suzi felt sorry for him. He'd admitted things weren't easy. He must be dreadfully torn between wanting Tom to be happy and wanting to make a clean break from Wynona. Softly she said, 'Maybe that's what friends are for. Do you want to talk about it? It might seem better if you share your worries.' She'd try her best to get things back to normal.

'No, I don't want to spoil our precious day together talking about Wynona. Now, eat up and let's go and see those Monets you said you were interested in. Unless you'd like a pudding of some sort first. They've got a lovely gooey assortment on the counter.'

Suzi flashed Cameron a smile of encouragement as he was trying so hard to please her. 'Maybe later,' she murmured. 'I'm hoping to get some ideas for the scenery I'm painting at school.'

'I read the letter. Now that *is* something I could be involved with as I imagine most parents will be helping after they get back from work.'

'That's right, we're going to do it in the evenings. It would be good if you could join us, but what about Tom?'

'I've talked to Dorcas and she's happy to keep him for longer or even take him home and put him to bed. What exactly will we be painting?'

'It's all quite complicated as we need an outside scene which takes place in a wood and a scene in a kitchen and we need to be able to change the scenery round quite quickly. I've done some sketches, but I've still got a few problems with the technical details of some of it.'

'Maybe you'd let me have a look and see if a fresh pair of eyes can come up with the answers.'

'That would be good.' She stood up and waited as Cameron returned the tray to the clear away trolley and they carried on their voyage of discovery around the various exhibits.

Suzi was overwhelmed by the treasures at the gallery and knew that she would have to visit again. Cameron chatted, teased her and made her laugh and she felt a connection with him. No, she must stop thinking that. Then she remembered that, although she never wanted to be disloyal to Matt, she had decided to move forward and maybe her friendship with Cameron would help her do just that.

Content and drained they dragged themselves away at closing time and headed across the square to the station. Suzi had thoroughly enjoyed her day out with Cameron. Despite the disagreement while they were having lunch, they'd got on well and she'd learned more about his creative side.

Outside, the pavements were slippery from a recent shower and it seemed only natural that Cameron should take Suzi's hand to prevent her tripping. She wished they lived on the edge of the world so they could carry on like that for ever; she felt a warmth and security which she hadn't felt for a long time.

All too soon, they were home and Cameron delved in his pocket for the key.

'Mind the hamster doesn't get you,' he whispered, as they went inside.

Suzi giggled, but as she was reminded of Honey's presence, she said, 'I'd better just check that she has enough water. Shall I put her upstairs with me? Does her scrabbling disturb you?' She felt it might help Cameron relax more easily if he had no responsibilities whilst Tom was away with his grandparents.

'Don't worry so much. She's fine. Being in the dining room we shut the door at night and neither of us hears a thing. She's quite a sweet little thing.

Even Mum and Dad spent time stroking her and talking to her this morning. Hurry back and keep me company. It's been a wonderful day.' Cameron stood close to Suzi and looked her in the eye. She was loath to pull her gaze away. It had indeed been a wonderful day and she hoped it wasn't over yet. She was glad they'd been able to get over their difficult time during lunch.

She flicked off her shoes which were rubbing her heels into blisters and went off to see Honey. 'Cameron,' she called urgently, 'she's gone. There's no sign of her.' The cage door was ajar, the food and water looked untouched and there were no scratching noises.

Cameron came up behind her and put his hands on her shoulders. 'Don't worry, she must be around somewhere. How on earth did she get out?'

Suzi was exasperated. A furry animal was standing between her and a blissful evening with the man she was falling in love with, despite her resolution to keep emotionally uninvolved. 'Tom must have left the cage open,' she replied.

As soon as she said it, she felt Cameron's hands stiffen. 'Why do you think it was Tom's fault? We were all fussing around Honey and the cage this morning, even his nana and granddad.'

'Hamsters don't escape by themselves, Cameron,' she responded. 'What do you think happened, then?' She was cross with herself. Whatever was she thinking of? She took a deep breath and pressed her lips together hoping she wouldn't say anything else inflammatory.

Calmly, he turned her round so she was facing him. 'I don't know what happened. I just don't like anyone to be blamed for something they may not have done, that's all, especially when that someone isn't around to have their say.'

Suzi felt mortified. He was right, of course he was. She took a deep breath and apologised, for which she was rewarded by a quick kiss on the cheek.

'So let's get hamster hunting,' he grinned.

The situation was diffused and Suzi was determined that it would stay that way.

Precious minutes ticked by and there was no sign of Honey. They tried tempting her out from wherever she was with titbits of food, clucking noises and whistling. Eventually, when Suzi was just about ready to admit defeat and put 'hamster' on the shopping list for the next day, they heard scrabbling behind a cupboard. Luckily, it was freestanding and could be moved out without too much trouble.

'Put the cage in the corner with the door facing the cupboard and I'll move the cupboard out as slowly as I can and hopefully, she'll run straight home.'

Suzi doubted the ease with which this rescue attempt could be made, but as she had nothing better to suggest, she carried out Cameron's instructions. To the surprise of both of them, it worked like a dream. Honey seemed as amazed as they did and quickly settled down under an untidy mound of shredded paper.

Suzi and Cameron were on their hands and knees with a hamster cage between them. Cameron's jovial chuckles were infectious and soon Suzi and he were giggling over the ridiculousness of it.

'We ought to take a picture,' spluttered Cameron. 'Show Tom what we got up to when he wasn't around.' Then he grew serious and their eyes met. This time there would be no pulling away, no excuses. They came as close together as they were able over the cage and their eager lips would soon meet for the first time. On the brink of this breathtaking experience, Suzi wanted to remember it for ever. Then the phone rang and the mood was dispelled.

'You'll have to get it, Suzi, I'm a bit stuck behind this thing.' Cameron indicated Honey's cage and the cupboard. 'It'll probably be Tom.'

'Hi, Tom, Mum Two here,' giggled Suzi into the phone. Then she pursed her lips and replaced the receiver. 'Odd.'

'Wasn't it Tom?'

'It was a woman. I couldn't hear what she was saying because the line was a bit crackly. I'm sure she'll get in touch again if it's urgent.'

Cameron had by this time extricated himself from behind the furniture. He surveyed her with steely eyes, but said nothing. Suzi knew their chance of a special moment had passed and she was disappointed. But perhaps it was all for the best as she knew she should wait until Cameron was completely free, legally anyway, from Wynona. She stood up and brushed herself down, dislodging some shreds of paper from the capture of Honey. 'I'll go and write up my notes about the art gallery,' she said, 'while they're still fresh in my mind.'

'I think I'll watch television. You can join me if you like.' But Cameron didn't push the invitation or sound as if he really wanted her to stay now. Maybe he'd also reminded himself that there was no way they could be close at the moment. She should respect him for not taking advantage of her growing feelings for him. All of a sudden she realised why Cameron's mood had changed. The woman on the phone could well have been Wynona and Cameron, realising this, was now worried and wondering why she had called.

'No, it's all right,' said Suzi, dully. With an aching heart, she slowly made her way to her flat torturing herself with wondering what would have happened if the phone hadn't rung.

7

In the morning, Suzi crept down the stairs hoping to get her few bits of household shopping and not disturb Cameron. He, however, was already up and as she came down the stairs, apologised to Suzi as she side-stepped his boxes and packages in the hall. 'I'm having a clear out,' he explained. 'I was awake early so decided to get up and do something useful before work. Probably most of this stuff should be put out for the bin men or else taken to the refuse tip.'

'Are you a hoarder, too?' she asked, remembering all the belongings still at her parents' house waiting to be gone through. 'I can't bear to throw things away.'

Cameron laughed, 'And when you do, you always need them?'

Suzi smiled her agreement with what

he said. She made her tortuous way to the front door and glanced back. 'Hey, some of those look like paintings. Did you do them?' When Cameron's features reddened and he hesitated with his unpacking, Suzi was convinced. 'May I look at them? Please.'

After wavering a little, Cameron shrugged his shoulders. 'If you like, I suppose so.'

Eagerly, Suzi pulled off the cloth protecting them and stood back to get the full view of Cameron's works of art. There were at least a dozen and she took her time inspecting them.

Cameron fidgeted. 'You don't have to be polite. I'm no genius.'

Suzi's eyes flickered from the canvases to Cameron. 'They're wonderful,' she breathed. 'So lifelike.' She'd wondered how good an artist Cameron was, but she'd never believed him to be this talented. At once she felt ashamed of undermining him if only to herself.

Cameron sat on the bottom stair and turned the top canvas towards him.

'That was done during a holiday before we had Tom. I had so much more time then.'

Suzi continued to scour through the pile. 'Are there any of you here?'

'Not worth studying, I assure you,' he said, with a grimace.

'Oh, Cameron, don't be so modest,' smiled Suzi. 'I'll find them if I carry on through these.'

'No, please don't,' Cameron snapped, throwing the cloth back over the collection. 'You were on your way out, weren't you?'

Suzi knew he'd closed up again, but what she'd said to make him do that she had no idea. 'I'm sorry,' she whispered, knowing she'd upset him, but not knowing how.

Immediately, Cameron crossed the narrow hallway to her. 'I didn't mean to shout, it's just that . . . ' He reached behind him, tore back the protective cloth once more and produced two canvases, holding them up. A deep flush of red suffused his cheeks. 'Now you know why I didn't want you to look at them. I've no idea why I hung on to them.'

Suzi was appalled. Both pictures were of Cameron, but his handsome features had been slashed with something sharp and holes had been gouged where his eyes should have been. 'I don't understand.'

He didn't look Suzi in the face, glancing down at his feet instead. 'Wynona did it. She came home one night and I asked her if she'd had a good time. Honestly, that's all I did. But it was enough to make her rage. These,' he nodded at the pile, 'were up on the wall of the house we lived in. I waited until she'd gone to bed and then I took them all down. I didn't want Tom to know about the incident. I bundled the paintings away and then the removal men just put them in the container. I should have got rid of them. Anyway, here they are and it's time they went.' He reached for the cloth to cover up the hideous reminder of the heartlessness of his wife.

Suzi put an arm around him and hugged him gently. 'How awful for you.' Taking her by surprise, Cameron responded by enveloping her in his eager arms. She laid her head against his chest and felt his fingers push through her hair. Holding her face up to his, desperately wanting to feel his lips on hers, their eyes met and they pulled apart.

'I'm sorry, Suzi, you're such an attractive and loving woman, but I shouldn't have given in to my feelings. Will you forgive me?'

Suzi was cross with herself for allowing this to happen. She should have maintained a decent distance from Cameron, even though a tiny part of her was thrilled that he might just feel something for her after all. Embarrassed, they stared at the slashed paintings. Then Suzi said, 'Forget it.' She wanted to do anything but forget the feelings aroused in her during the brief moment of closeness. She tried to regain her composure. 'I've got a suggestion, but I don't know what you'll think. You could get rid of the two damaged ones and put the others up around the house. I'm sure Tom would like it. He could even put up some of his. What do you say?'

'I'm not sure,' replied Cameron, moving away from her to pick up a painting.

'They'd look great on the walls of the sitting room or up the stairs. I'll help you arrange them if you like.'

Cameron checked his watch. 'I'm already late. This has taken more time than I thought. You could do it,' he smiled, looking apologetic.

'I'd love to if you're sure you don't mind.' A nod and a smile from Cameron was all she needed to take on the task. Not wanting to go shopping now, Suzi set to work. Suzi was shocked by the cruel side of Wynona. Luckily Tom had been spared the sight of his father's paintings being disfigured. She'd make sure she presented the others well and she hoped there was going to be enough room for them.

All the pictures were standing up against the walls of the hall so that she could have a good look at them, when she heard the key turn in the lock. Surprised, she looked up. It was Cameron. He'd only been gone a short while.

'I've decided to take the day off. I'll put in some time on the computer this evening. I wasn't sure if you could hammer a nail in straight.' Cameron beamed at her.

About to be indignant at his lack of faith in her ability as a picture hanger, Suzi realised he was joking.

'I wasn't even sure you'd recognise a hammer. Tools and nails are in the shed. I've got us some lunch.' He held up a supermarket bag. 'I'll just pop things in the fridge and then we can get busy.'

Suzi wandered out to the shed to collect what they'd need. The project had now trebled in appeal with the addition of Cameron's company and lunch thrown in.

Having decided the best spot for each painting, Suzi placed the steps in position. 'I'll hang the first one, shall I? Just to show you how capable I am.' She was aware of Cameron holding the steps firmly as she climbed them carefully and banged in the nail. She was glad that it went in perfectly straight. With the painting now hanging on the wall, they both stood back and admired it.

'I'm fond of snow scenes. It reminds me of childhood winters. I hope Tom will have happy memories of his childhood.' Cameron sounded wistful.

'Of course he will. You mustn't doubt your abilities as a father. From what I've seen it's obvious you love Tom very much.' Suzi handed him a nail, 'Now it's your turn.' Suzi laughed when Cameron's nail bent as he bashed it in. 'That's what's known as divine retribution. Here, why don't you pull that nail out with these pliers and let me knock the nails in?' Suzi passed Cameron the pliers.

Suzi enjoyed doing something practical to help Cameron and was pleased that she'd suggested the pictures on the wall. He seemed satisfied with the suggestion too. He'd even taken time off work to be involved with it. Not for a moment did she believe he was really checking up on her.

'You've a good eye,' said Cameron. 'I'd never have thought of putting those two together.' He gestured towards a bleak moor and a seaside scene.

'I think it's the colours I was looking at more than content. They do look good, don't they? I wonder if Tom would like some of his paintings on the wall. I know he had some on the fridge in Scotland, but a change might be a good thing.'

'You seem to know a lot about Tom and his time with Mum and Dad. What else did he tell you?' Cameron held out a hand as Suzi descended the steps.

'Nothing really. Only that his nana

stuck his school pictures on the fridge with a magnet. He thought it was very clever that they didn't fall down.' Suzi smiled at the memory of Tom and her in the classroom that day. He really was a changed little boy now and she was pleased for both him and his father.

They moved on to the walls in the sitting room. The décor was light and airy and Suzi had picked out pictures to complement it, making sure the relaxed atmosphere remained intact.

'Nearly done,' Cameron said looking round the sitting room. 'If you can hang these last two small ones I'll go and get lunch started.'

Moments later he was back. 'I forgot the bread. I'll just nip out and fetch some.'

'It's all right, Cameron, I don't mind, really.' Suzi didn't want him going to a lot of trouble which she suspected was just for her.

'It's all right,' he smiled. 'I won't be long.' He rushed out of the house and she continued with her picture hanging.

Suzi had hung the paintings, tidied up and was just wondering where Cameron had got to when she became aware of rain pounding on the window. Hearing the front door open she wandered into the hall to be met by a soaked Cameron. He went straight into the kitchen and slung the bread down on the worktop. Suzi felt uncomfortable that he'd put himself out and had got drenched. She followed him into the kitchen and held out a towel for him to wipe his dripping face and hair.

'I'll have to change. Look at me.'

Suzi did and, through the now transparent fabric of his white shirt, she glimpsed his body, hard muscles rippling as he vigorously rubbed at his wet hair.

'Sorry about this,' he grinned, not looking sorry at all.

Suzi stared after him as he bounded up the stairs to get into dry clothes. His broad back and shoulders reminded her of the painting of Samson in the gallery.

Cameron too was, quite simply, beautiful.

Trying to distract herself she fussed around the kitchen, hoping she was getting out the things Cameron had bought for lunch.

When he reappeared the only sign of his soaking was his still wet hair.

'This cheese is delicious,' declared Suzi nibbling a piece of strong Cheddar and breaking off a chunk of the fresh bread Cameron had gone out to fetch. 'Definitely worth getting wet for,' she smiled as she passed the french stick to him.

'Not the most imaginative lunch, is it? But the atmosphere is perfect.' He waved his piece of bread towards the sitting room. 'I can't thank you enough for creating a nice homely feel to the place. It was a bit cold, wasn't it?'

'It's nice to have personal things around,' stated Suzi, aware that she didn't have many of her own upstairs in her flat. She decided she'd remedy that as soon as possible.

They finished their lunch and Cameron said, 'I'll put the kettle on, unless you'd prefer some fruit juice?'

'Coffee would be great,' replied Suzi. 'Are there any more jobs we could do?'

Cameron shook his head. 'You've done more than enough already. But I've an idea. I've been to your workplace, how do you fancy visiting mine? I'd like to show you my portfolio for the latest project we're working on. It's one of the main line stations in London which is being totally renovated, but keeping the original features. It's going to look fantastic, both inside and out. It's very exciting.'

Suzi could tell that he was passionate about his work and was delighted to be invited to his office. 'That's a great idea, but I thought you'd decided not to go in today.'

'That was because of the possibility of bent nails.' He grinned at her before becoming serious again. 'Let's drop those ruined paintings off at the tip first. I don't want there to be any possibility of Tom seeing them. You don't mind doing that, do you?'

She didn't mind at all and was pleased at how satisfied Cameron looked when he'd slung the pictures into the skip with all the other household rubbish. 'There,' he said, 'a nasty reminder from my past gone. Good riddance!'

Suzi was always fascinated by the other travellers when she was on the tube. She enjoyed people watching and tried to imagine what people did and how they were related to each other. But today she wondered what someone noticing the two of them would be thinking. They were both dressed casually. Would people think they were on a day out? Might they think they were colleagues, relations or friends? Even landlord and tenant? She smiled. Then she noticed that Cameron was watching her reflection in the window across from them. She turned and smiled at him. Husband and wife? She twisted her engagement and wedding rings. She hadn't been thinking so much about Matt recently she realised guiltily. He'd been constantly on her mind until she'd met Cameron. Even her mother had noticed how taken she was with him and she'd barely said a word.

Strangely, the previous evening she'd taken out the box of newspaper cuttings she'd kept about Matt. There were several from incidents before he'd died, including a humorous one about a cat rescue. But she also had all the articles she'd found about the last flat fire. And there was mention of his bravery award which had been presented to her. She could barely remember the ceremony as she'd been in a fug of grief at the time. She'd read every word again and then carefully replaced the cuttings. After tying a ribbon round the box she'd put it at the back of her wardrobe.

Cameron's office was a big nod to modernity. The reception area was all glass with huge trees in tubs. 'Wow,' was all Suzi could manage. She was surprised to realise this was the place Cameron hurried off to each day after taking Tom to Dorcas. She hadn't considered what his place of work would look like. They took the lift which being on the outside of the building gave them a wonderful view of London. When they reached Cameron's floor he took her hand and led her past colleagues working at their computer stations to his work area by the windows. 'Look at that view,' Suzi exclaimed. 'I don't know how you ever get any work done.'

'It is amazing, isn't it? Do you want to look at my work in progress? I'm responsible for the concourse where the food outlets are. This is how I envisage it.' He pointed to the computer screen.

'Goodness.' Suzi had never imagined a London train station to have such a continental look.

'That's just to give an idea of what it should look like. The plans are all here.' Cameron opened a folder on the computer and showed her the list of contents.

'I wouldn't understand what those are all about, but this representation is really good. Look at all these people sitting outside the café.'

'Do you recognise anyone?' Cameron asked grinning.

Suzi looked more closely. There was a boy at one of the tables with a glass of something. 'It's Tom! And you've put yourself with him, and there's a woman.' The suspicion that it might be Wynona annoyed her until she reminded herself it had nothing to do with her. But Cameron's next words were unexpected.

'That's you, Suzi. I hope that when it's completed we'll be able to go together. Although Tom will probably be a teenager by the time the project is finished. I also had a look at the scenery sketches for the school production and sorted out those technical problems you had. Let me show you. If you scroll down you'll see all my suggestions.

How about I fetch us some coffee and when you've finished on the computer you can enjoy the view while I send off a couple of emails.'

Suzi watched him walk back down the office and saw the easy way he had with his co-workers. He was a man of many layers it would seem: a loving, practical and amusing father as well as a professional and popular work colleague. When he returned he passed her a steaming cup and said, 'They all want to know who the gorgeous woman I'm with is.'

'Very funny, don't tease me.'

Cameron looked serious. 'I'm not teasing you, you are gorgeous.'

'What did you say?'

'That you're my friend, my best friend.'

Suzi was happy with that and sipped her coffee contentedly.

* * *

Having made Cameron's house more homely by hanging the pictures Suzi was determined to make her flat equally inviting. She took a few of the postcards she'd bought at the gallery at the end of her day out with Cameron and mounted them on coloured card to make a very effective collage. Having framed the resulting picture she hung it from a nail and stood back to admire her effort. Another idea came to her. She would produce a couple of sketches and use those to decorate her flat as well. She would have liked to repeat the sketch she'd made of Cameron in the classroom, but instead decided to do one of Tom and one of Honey. The drawing of Tom came easily and she soon had a lifelike picture, but to draw Honey she would need to have the subject in front of her. She borrowed Honey one afternoon when no one else was in the house and was pleased with the resulting picture of a very sleepy hamster.

Suzi had mixed feelings when she went back to school after the half term break. Since her time alone with

Cameron, she'd hardly seen him as he'd been working long hours and then spending time with Tom. She consoled herself with the thought that he'd called her his best friend. She couldn't want more than that.

To use her time effectively she'd taken her project file into the garden and filled it with some good plans for making lessons informative and fun. They would come in useful in the weeks ahead when she was going to be thrown in at the deep end with the older children.

She wandered around the classroom looking forward to seeing the children again and hearing about their break. No doubt Tom would have plenty to say about his nana and granddad. Suzi smiled as she remembered the happy little boy who returned from Brighton and was delighted with the gallery of pictures in the house. He'd come up to tell her especially and said that Nana and Granddad thought the display was splendid. He'd also been pleased with her sketches of him and Honey displayed on her wall. 'I'd like a picture of Honey,' he'd said. 'I haven't any pictures on my walls.'

'Okay, you can have this one if you do a drawing of Honey for me to replace it.' So now she had her drawing of Tom next to his drawing of Honey.

'Hi, Mrs Warner, where are you? Miles away by the look of it.'

Suzi came out of her reverie and saw Dorcas smiling broadly at her.

'Dorcas, how lovely to see you. How are you?' She nodded towards Dorcas's growing tummy. 'You're always so cheerful and you've got such energy,' admired Suzi. 'You'll have to let me know your secret.'

'Love,' whispered Dorcas, a giggle exploding from her. 'Talking of which, how did you and that gorgeous man get on over half term?'

'He is still married, as you well know,' replied Suzi, primly.

'Not for much longer. He's almost a free agent.'

'Sorry, I can't talk now, I'd better start the school day. We'll get together soon for a catch up.'

Dorcas took the hint and left the classroom. Suzi waited until the children had settled and asked them what they'd done in the half term holiday.

Tom's hand shot up. 'Please, Miss, I went to Brighton with my nana and granddad.' He turned to the class and explained. 'That's the seaside. We had ice cream and Granddad dropped his and Nana told him off. Then one day we had fish and chips on the beach. They were yummy. I had a lovely time and then when I got home Dad took me to a gallery place. It was quite boring, but he liked it when he went before. He went with a very nice person he said. And anyway, my mum's coming to see me soon and she's going to stay at my house. She's coming from America. Next weekend.'

Tom paused for breath and Suzi could have done with breathing space, too. That was a lot to take in. Cameron had described her to his son as a very nice person. But the edge was taken off that piece of information as she was hit with the news that Wynona was coming to stay. She didn't know how she'd react to Tom's mother especially knowing the way she'd behaved at times. Maybe she could keep out of the way and avoid seeing her altogether. She was also puzzled that Cameron hadn't mentioned the visit to her, especially after his revelation that she, Suzi, was his best friend.

* * *

After a hectic morning Suzi was pleased to have the lunchtime interval in which to unwind a little. She decided to skip lunch and have a walk around the block in order to refresh her mind. It was a beautiful summer's day and flowers were blooming everywhere, but her mind was on other things. She didn't think she could bear seeing Cameron with Wynona or to hear Tom calling her

'Mummy'. Realising there was not a thing she could do about it she tried to tell herself not to be silly. There was precious little evidence that Cameron thought of her, Suzi, as anyone more than his tenant, friend and Tom's schoolteacher, but if that were so, why had he taken her in his arms and been about to kiss her just a few days ago? And why had he missed work so that they could hang paintings together? Her head thumped and tears threatened. She knew she was being ridiculous and must try and put her feelings to one side. Resolutely, she swallowed hard and returned to school.

Mr Tanner knocked on the window as he saw her approach the school entrance. Smiling, he beckoned her into his office. 'Suzi, good holiday? Remember our little chat? I'd like you to take Year Five this afternoon. Melanie's gone home ill so I thought if you take her class I'll take yours. It will be good for me to get to know your little ones better.'

Suzi welcomed the change. It would keep her on her toes and her mind occupied. She went to her classroom and took the project folder from her desk drawer and thumbed through it before deciding exactly what she would do.

When the final bell rang, the children fled home, leaving Suzi shattered.

'What're you doing in here?' Dorcas materialised. 'You look dreadful. Tom said you were with Year Five. They can be a bunch of perishers.'

'Some of them are a bit of a handful, but I can see some of the others going places. I've got an idea, but I need to talk to the children's parents and Cameron before I say anything more.'

'Sounds intriguing, but forget school now. You need some TLC. Get your stuff and come home with me.'

Without a word of protest, Suzi did just that.

* * *

159

Suzi sat at Dorcas's kitchen table while the children played out in her overgrown garden. 'Wynona's coming home,' she said, getting the news in quickly knowing that Dorcas would pounce, wanting to know what was up.

'Oh yes, I know that,' said Dorcas, topping up Suzi's mug of tea and cutting her another enormous slice of lemon cake. 'Is that what's troubling you? It doesn't mean a thing. From what Cameron's said they'll never be reconciled.'

'Possibly not, but she might cause problems. She might unsettle Tom and Cameron.'

'I don't think she'll be unsettling Cameron except in a practical way. From what he's said to me the sooner that divorce comes through the better. Between you and me,' she bent forward, her bangles jangling, 'I don't think Cameron knew what he was letting himself in for. He opened up to me one day when he collected Tom. He thought he was madly in love with

Wynona otherwise he wouldn't have married her, but he soon realised his mistake. He tried hard to make it work, but realised she wasn't bothered about their relationship anymore.' She paused and took a bite of cake. 'I think he definitely prefers you. He told me about your smashing time together and what a lovely companion you were. Well, are, I suppose he must mean because he says that it's really nice having you around the house and he wishes he saw more of you, but he's been so busy he's hardly seen you. There I've told you far too much.'

Attempting a smile, Suzi wished she knew how to resolve her anguish. She wasn't looking forward to Wynona's arrival at the weekend.

8

Suzi immediately recognised the light tap on her door. Before it was fully open she said, 'Hello, Tom.'

The little boy walked in, grinning. 'My mum's coming today. I'm going to see if I can have a pet. Do you think she'll say yes?'

'I don't know, Tom, it's quite a responsibility having a pet. But you have reminded me of something. I've printed out those photos we took of Honey when she was staying with us. Here they are. I like this one best of you and your dad with Honey.' Suzi had resisted printing a copy for herself.

'Can I have them? To keep?'

'I did them for you.' She tucked the photos in an envelope and gave them to Tom.

'Thanks. I'd like to make a thing like that with the photos,' he said nodding to Suzi's postcard collage.

'I'll help you if you like. Maybe one weekend.'

'Mum might help me today.'

'That would be good.' Suzi wasn't as confident as Tom seemed to be that Wynona would help him. From what Cameron had told her, it wasn't likely.

'Dad said don't be long. I've got to tidy my room for Mum.' He pulled a face. 'I don't think she'll come in my bedroom so I don't see why I should.'

'You know you must do what your dad says. Off you go.'

'Will you come and see my mum? You can be *her* friend, too. You're Dad's friend and my friend so you can be Mummy's friend as well.'

'I'm not sure I'll have time to meet your mummy. I've got quite a lot to do today and I might go shopping.' She ushered him out of the door. 'Have a great time.'

'I expect my mum's got me a present. I haven't seen her for ages. I'll come and show you later. I'll let you play with it.' He skipped off down the stairs, stopping halfway to give her a little wave.

Suzi sank on the settee. Where could she go to be out of the way? She couldn't bear to meet the woman who had so cruelly destroyed Cameron's paintings, but worse than that the woman who didn't seem to have maternal feelings for her adorable son. But then why should she leave her home just because Wynona was coming? Defiantly she decided to stay in and concentrate on her paperwork.

She was busy filling in the children's record sheets when there was another light knock at the door.

'Come in, you little rascal,' she called.

Cameron laughed as he came into the room. 'Hello there. Busy?'

'Very. I thought you were my favourite boy.' She flushed with embarrassment. 'I mean Tom,' she explained unnecessarily.

'I gathered that term of endearment

wasn't meant for me. I've come to ask you a favour. Wynona needs to talk to me in private and Tom's being difficult. He says he's not going anywhere out of the house while his mummy's here so I can't ask Dorcas.'

'It's fine, I'm very happy to have him. I've nearly finished my work anyway and I haven't anything else I need to do. We can bake some biscuits. But I imagine Wynona will want him back pretty quickly as she hasn't seen him for so long.'

Cameron made a face. 'She's not what you'd call motherly. She knows it and I think feels quite guilty. It's just not part of her make up. I think some women are like that.'

'Yes, I suppose so. Send him up then. I'll try to keep him occupied here. Leave the door ajar so that he can just walk in.'

Tom wasn't the happy boy she'd seen earlier that morning. 'I showed Mum the photos of Honey and she said 'Who's that?' pointing at you and I said

165

you are my friend and she was cross. Dad said it was none of her business. She said my dad's been playing.'

'Well, he has been playing with you, hasn't he?' Suzi wanted to cheer him up, and was pleased he hadn't understood that Wynona had accused Cameron of playing around. 'Did you make the collage together? Using the photos I gave you.'

'No, Mum didn't want to. She said it's not her thing.'

'I'm still happy to help you with that sometime.'

'Yeah.' Poor Tom looked so defeated.

'Did she say you can have a pet?' Suzi asked, hoping to steer the conversation on to something else.

'No, she didn't listen when I told her. She was texting someone. She gave me this card and said I can get something expensive with that. She didn't bring me a present. She didn't have time to shop. She said she'd been too busy with work and something about Daddy not giving her enough money. I don't get grown-ups. Why didn't she bring me something? I wouldn't have minded if it had been little, like a mouse.'

Tom was on the verge of tears. Surely Wynona could have found the time to buy something for her own son. She swallowed her anger and smiled at Tom. 'That's a gift voucher she's given you — you can choose whatever you like with that.'

His face lit up. 'Can I choose a puppy?'

'Well, no, I didn't quite mean whatever you like, but maybe you could get a toy puppy, rather than a real one. We'll look on the internet and we'll see what there is that you might like. We'll tell your dad later when you've chosen something and see if he agrees it's a good choice.'

'I don't want something, I want a pet. It's not fair. Olivia has Bandit.'

Suzi saw again the unhappy boy who had started school at the beginning of term. She desperately hoped they weren't going to have to begin all over again. 'I know. Here, come and sit beside me and I'll tell you a story about a little boy and his pet hamster who was an escapologist.'

Tom's eyes widened. 'A what?'

Tom was entranced by the story, but Suzi was increasingly worried about the raised voices coming from downstairs.

'Let's put some music on and do some baking,' she suggested.

'But you haven't finished the story. It's an exciting bit too. Please Suzi, tell me the rest.'

She knew she'd have to be firm if she didn't want him to hear the argument going on. It was mainly Wynona's voice she could hear. 'I'll finish the story when we've got some home-made biscuits to eat.' She went into the kitchen, switched the radio on and started sorting out ingredients. 'Come and wash your hands and we'll get started.'

'What's that noise? It sounds like my mummy. I want to go and see.' Tom headed for the door.

'No wait! Tom you must understand. Mummy and Daddy don't see each other very much and they have a lot of things to talk about. You can go down later, I promise and you know I never break promises.'

Reluctantly, Tom made his way to the kitchen and reached to wash his hands. For a while it seemed as if the awkward moments had been deflected and Tom pummelled the doughy mixture enthusiastically after carefully weighing out the ingredients under Suzi's supervision. 'Can I taste some?' he asked pulling off a small piece and raising it to his mouth.

'Why not wait until you've finished and then scrape out the bowl? That's what I used to do when I helped with the baking at home,' replied Suzi thinking of her mother and the happy times they'd spent together. Childhood was very precious and disappeared so quickly. Tom arranged lumps of the mixture on a baking tray and then set about sampling the leftovers.

With the biscuits in the oven and Tom happily standing on a stool supposedly washing up, but making as many bubbles as he could, Suzi felt it was a good opportunity to go to the bathroom. When she returned there was no sign of Tom. Heading down the stairs she found him on the landing leaning over listening intently to his parents' conversation.

'Come back,' she whispered, but Tom ignored her.

'Dmitri's had his kids, they're grown up and he doesn't want another one to look after. Tom stays here with you as far as I'm concerned. I don't want him to come over for holidays. I'll see him when I'm over in England on business, I suppose.' Wynona's drawl carried clearly.

'You can't just abandon your son.'

'Watch me, Cameron, just watch me. Have I not made myself clear? I can't manage him. I just don't know how to deal with him. I don't want to see him.'

Suzi hugged Tom, picked him up and

carried him back up the stairs. Once in her flat she closed the door and eased him down into a chair. He wouldn't disentangle himself and sobbed into her shoulder.

Suzi couldn't believe what they'd just heard. How could any mother be like that about their child? She knew Tom was heartbroken, but also knew she wasn't the person best able to help him. 'I think you need to talk to your daddy. You wait here and I'll get him.' Suzi was furious with both Wynona and Cameron for allowing their son to hear their argument. They were both aware that he wasn't far away and they must have known their raised voices would carry. She rushed down the stairs and shouted at Cameron, 'You'd better get upstairs quickly. Tom heard what Wynona said about not wanting him.' She glared at Wynona.

'But you were supposed to be looking after him,' Cameron protested.

'And you're supposed to be responsible adults. Don't blame me for your mistakes. You've got a very unhappy child upstairs who needs you both.'

'So this is the girlfriend. Fiery isn't she? I thought you'd be looking for a more subdued type after your experience with me.' Wynona smirked. 'I'll be getting off then. Tell Tom goodbye. You two had better go and play at being Mom and Pop, but just remember you'll only be Mum Two in my boy's eyes.' With that she stormed out of the house.

Suzi clamped her mouth shut and watched Cameron bound up the stairs two at a time calling to Tom. Suzi followed close behind.

'Where is he?' Cameron demanded.

'What do you mean, where is he?' Suzi was aghast when she reached her flat. 'Whatever's happened to him? He was here just a moment ago. Maybe he's gone to his room.' She followed Cameron down a floor, but by the time she got to Tom's room Cameron was standing in the doorway looking stunned.

'He's not here either. I trusted you to look after him, Suzi. We'd better search the whole house. You do your flat, I'll start on this floor then we'll meet downstairs. Hurry, we've got to find him quickly and get this sorted. Wynona never was one to keep her feelings to herself, but she's surpassed anything I thought she was capable of. She's just so selfish, and arrogant enough to think everyone will kow-tow to her. I did tell you she was impossible. Perhaps now you understand the situation a little better.'

Suzi was devastated. As she quickly turned off the oven, she tormented herself with the thought that she shouldn't have left Tom when he'd been so upset. He *must* be in her flat. When Cameron had said he'd trusted her he hadn't said it with any malice, it had just been a statement of fact, but Suzi felt deeply hurt and longed with all her heart to find Tom safe. By the time she got to the ground floor Cameron's expression was grim. 'He's not in the house,' he said. 'We'd better search the garden and shed. If we don't find him there I'm calling the police.'

As they searched, Suzi racked her brains to think where a six-year old might go for comfort. Dorcas! Of course. He must be there. She rushed back into the house and pressed Dorcas's number into the phone.

'Fred? Is Tom with you?'

'No, it's the weekend. Whatever's the matter? You sound frantic. You must know he doesn't come at weekends.'

'But has he turned up unexpectedly?'

'Not that I know of. Cameron hasn't brought him so why would he be here? What's going on?' Fred sounded concerned.

'Please start searching. He's gone missing. Check everywhere. I'll be round straight away to help.' Suzi ended the call, her mind racing.

Cameron was standing in the doorway, looking bleak. 'We'll have to call the police.'

'Let me go round to Dorcas's first. I

can't bear hanging around not doing anything. I think he might be there. It's a place of safety and comfort for him. You wait here just in case he turns up. I'll let you know as soon as we've searched there.'

The look of utter misery on Cameron's face made Suzi determined she would find Tom if it was the last thing she did. She raced out of the house, not even bothering to shut the door behind her.

★   ★   ★

Dorcas and Fred were waiting at the open door when Suzi arrived at their house. Dorcas immediately gave Suzi a hug. 'He's not here. We've searched the whole house from top to bottom. I'm sorry. Did he run away? If so, whatever happened to make him do that? I'm sorry, Suzi, you can tell me later. For now we must just think where else he could be. Let's hope he's not hurt.'

Suzi's knees felt weak. She'd never

forgive herself if anything happened to Tom.

'Come in and sit down, we'll let Cameron know then try to think of anywhere else he might be. I wonder if he's gone to the house of one of his school friends. Somewhere he's been for tea. Let me think.'

As Suzi sat in one of the armchairs she realised something was missing. 'Where's Bandit?'

'Yes, where *is* Bandit, Fred?' Dorcas demanded. 'I hadn't noticed he was missing with all this worry.'

'He's outside,' said Fred looking rather shamefaced. 'He asked to go out in the garden some time ago and I'm afraid I forgot and shut him out there. He'll be fine, it's hardly cold and it's not wet. He likes being in the garden anyway.'

Dorcas and Suzi simultaneously rushed for the back door.

'The den, they must be there. Tom loves that place. Please let him be there.' Dorcas hurried down the garden, Suzi racing behind her. The door was ajar and they were greeted by a tail-wagging Bandit. Curled up in a blanket was Tom fast asleep, his long lashes brushing his tear-stained cheeks.

Suzi had never felt such a relief. 'Thank goodness. Let's phone Cameron and tell him the good news,' Suzi whispered. 'It will be best if he's here when Tom wakes up. They've got a lot to discuss.'

Leaving Dorcas to keep an eye on Tom while he slept, Suzi tiptoed out of the den and made the call to an emotional Cameron.

★ ★ ★

It had been a long day. Suzi had kept out of the way once father and son were reunited, but then Tom had demanded the rest of the tale of Honey the escapologist for his bedtime story and Suzi was happy to oblige. Cameron sat on Tom's bed listening to the story.

'That's your lot,' Suzi said, exhausted by her day of strange occurrences.

'Aw, I want more. I bet she escapes again and again and again.'

'She might do, but it won't be this evening. I'll think of another adventure for her for another night. We all need some rest now, even Honey.'

After kisses and hugs, Cameron and Suzi were able to leave Tom on the verge of sleep.

'He doesn't seem too affected by his ordeal today, does he?' she asked.

'It's hard to say. I wish Wynona had never visited. I thought it was going to be the best thing for Tom to see her sometimes, but now I'm wondering if it will be. Would you like a drink?' Cameron said. 'I think you deserve an explanation. I'm afraid I've expected rather a lot of you today and it's not fair on you.' He handed Suzi a glass of wine. 'Wynona has a new man, Dmitri. He's her boss and she's being promoted. Typical Wynona behaviour.'

'You don't seem surprised.'

'No, I'm not, she's had other male friends before and I realised something was going on when I phoned her. I could hear a man's voice in the background.'

'I'm sorry.' Suzi could still feel the ache of Matt's death and imagined Cameron's pain on the break-up of his marriage. It must have been especially difficult with their child to think of. The fact that they had failed to provide a secure and stable home life for Tom must be very hurtful to someone as caring as Cameron.

'It's all okay. I fell out of love with her some time ago. I've accepted that although I'm not even sure I knew what love was then. It's Tom I feel for, but I think we can make a good life for ourselves. He's settled here really well and I've been happier recently than I was during all the years with Wynona. You might be able to guess why.' Cameron reached out and tenderly stroked Suzi's cheek. Then he

179

took her glass and placed it on the coffee table. He gave her a smouldering look, gently cupped her face in his hands before bringing his lips to meet hers in a long lingering kiss.

9

Cameron was uncomfortable when he pulled away from the kiss he'd yearned for. 'I'm sorry, Suzi, I still feel so raw after Wynona. I really care about you, but this is all happening too quickly. We're both still in the early stages of trying to move on from the past.'

'It's all right, really,' replied Suzi, but Cameron could tell she was upset.

'No it's not,' he said, 'but you must see that I have to be cautious. I think it would be best if we regard each other as friends only.'

'Of course, I understand completely,' said Suzi, avoiding his gaze.

Cameron turned her face to his. 'It's not what I want, but it's the right thing.'

To his delight Suzi said, 'It's not what I want either, Cameron.'

She looked so wounded that Cameron had to add, 'Perhaps we could see how things turn out, take it slowly.' He was rewarded with a tiny smile from her.

'As for regarding each other as friends, surely that goes without saying. I love being with you.' Suzi wrapped her arms round him and brushed Cameron's cheek with her lips, turning an awkward moment into a heart-warming one.

★　★　★

'Well now, Cameron, you look as if you've lost a fivepence piece and found a ten pound note,' crowed Dorcas, hooking her arm through his as they walked around her glorious garden.

Grinning, Cameron returned, 'More like a fifty pound note.'

Cocking her head on one side and grinning mischievously at him, she asked, 'Are you going to spill the beans?'

'You must know it's Suzi. It's all a bit difficult. After we'd found Tom at the weekend, we got a bit euphoric and ended up kissing.'

'Please spare my blushes.' Dorcas gurgled infectiously.

'However, to my shame, a vision of Wynona came into my mind and I broke away.'

'Oh, Cameron, how could you?' Dorcas sounded so frustrated with him that he felt he should explain.

'I wasn't thinking of Wynona in a good way. Just how disastrous it was for all of us — Wynona, Tom and me. I don't ever want anything like that to happen again.'

Cameron couldn't bear the thought of another terrible relationship causing Tom distress. He couldn't face it for himself either. Wynona had made him wary of getting involved with another woman even one as kind and caring as Suzi. He felt unable to trust his judgement any more.

Dorcas interrupted his thoughts. 'Suzi's a lovely person, Cameron, she wouldn't want things to go wrong for Tom.'

'Of course, you're right. I know that and I couldn't bear for her to be hurt either. So, although I am happy because I think that Suzi and I have feelings for each other, I also hope I haven't blown it by distancing myself from her. After I broke away, I tried to explain to Suzi that it wasn't her fault. She understood, at least she said she did. I think we both agree that we can't rush our relationship.'

'It's good that you're both putting Tom first, but don't neglect each other.'

'Tom was the best thing to come out of my marriage, you know. I don't think love figured highly, if at all. I imagined myself in love with Wynona, of course, or I'd never have asked her to marry me. I think instead of hearts and flowers she just saw dollar bills and a ladder going way, way up when she paid me any attention at all. Anyway, Dorcas, my marriage is finally over. Wynona's gone from my life. All I'm waiting for now is the piece of paper

184

making it official.'

'So have you told Suzi all this? Does she know about why you and Wynona split up? You really should tell her, Cameron, she's not a mind reader.' Dorcas tossed her hair and fixed him with a steely eye. 'I know you think I'm a bit scatty at times, but I'd fight tooth and nail for my family and that includes Suzi. Don't give her the runaround, Cameron. She deserves better than that. Exactly how do you feel about her?' Dorcas waited, but he didn't reply.

Cameron wasn't sure he wanted to talk to anyone regarding how he felt about Suzi. Not just yet. He wanted to savour it to himself and not put a jinx on what might turn out to be an amazing future for them both. As soon as he'd seen Suzi on Tom's first day in her class, he'd known there was something extraordinary about her. It was more than just the efficient way she'd eased Tom into his new school and more than the respect the headteacher so obviously had for her. Her beauty, which had initially attracted him, was more than skin deep. He longed to be with her and when he wasn't physically with her, he thought about her. She was all he ever wanted in a woman. But he had no right to pursue her. Also, he had no idea about Suzi's husband. For all he knew he might still be around; she'd never talked of him and Cameron wondered why not.

Dorcas broke into his thoughts. 'Wynona can't be completely gone from your life, though, can she? She'll want to be with Tom, won't she?'

Cameron gave Dorcas an affectionate squeeze. 'Not everyone's an earth mother like you,' he smiled. Then his look grew serious. 'I'd rather Wynona wasn't around. I'd prefer it to be just me and Tom for the time being.' The future was very uncertain still. He cleared his throat and continued. 'I want Tom to stay with me. I don't want him near Wynona. I'm sure that sounds harsh, but every time she has contact with him he gets upset. I've spent so long trying to give him security. He's been so happy these past weeks and a lot of it is because of you, Dorcas. I want to thank you very much for being there for him.'

'He's a gorgeous lad and he's had a lot to put up with. Bandit adores him, too. I'm not so sure that Olivia is always up there on a best buddy basis, although they've been getting on a bit better lately I have to admit.'

A chuckle of laughter escaped Cameron. He was pleased Dorcas had sidetracked the conversation. 'Can I ask you one thing?' he chanced.

'Ask away.'

'It's just that Suzi has never told me about her previous relationship. All along I've assumed she's single, by which I suppose she's divorced, separated, something like that. She hasn't told me what happened between her and Mr Warner.'

'Have you asked her?' Dorcas asked lightly, but her face lacked its usual sparkle.

Cameron ran his fingers through his hair and sighed. 'It seems so simple, doesn't it, but each time the subject's come up, it's as if it's not the right time.'

*　★　★*

When Cameron got home he let Tom watch the television while he took time to think about the devastating things Dorcas had told him about Suzi. On the one hand, he was pleased that she had no man around her, but on the other he didn't want her to have suffered so much. He groaned inwardly when he thought how he'd been short tempered with her when Tom was missing and when Honey escaped. He'd even reminded her that she was Mrs Warner. She must have been deeply hurt by his remarks.

Dorcas had said that it was up to the two of them to sort things out and she was sure it would all turn out for the best. Cameron supposed she was right.

188

'Hey, Tommy boy,' Cameron said, squatting down to Tom's level, 'you like Suzi, don't you?' Cameron couldn't get her out of his mind and wanted to talk about her to someone.

Tom didn't appear to want to take his eyes off the TV screen. He just replied, 'Why?'

'I just wondered. I thought we might do a few more things with her. But only if you'd like to.'

'Okay, I don't mind, I like her.' At last he took his eyes off the screen and put an arm around Cameron's neck. 'I wish Mummy liked me.'

Cameron hugged his son back, his heart breaking at the child's unhappiness. He vowed that Tom wouldn't be upset like that again if he could help it. Perhaps his initial reaction after kissing Suzi had been the right one. It would be better not to get drawn into a relationship with her. What would happen if he got involved with her, as he wanted to, and then she went off him further down the line? Tom would be hurt all over again. It wouldn't be fair. Although almost every instinct told him he was falling in love with Suzi, he knew he had to be careful. He'd vowed to put Tom first; it was the least the poor child deserved. He had been making good progress without Wynona until she'd turned up and soured things.

He'd make himself strong; he was all Tom had now. His parents adored him, of course, but they were a long way away. If it meant he'd have to distance himself from Suzi for Tom to be happy, then he'd do it. It wouldn't be easy, but he couldn't let his son down. In the meantime, he hoped that Suzi would get the message that they could only be friends; he didn't think he would be able to endure telling her directly.

★   ★   ★

The small group of children from Year Five were thrilled to be visiting Cameron at his office and had been excited on the tube journey chattering away and keeping Suzi entertained. On the first afternoon she'd taught them she'd realised that a couple of them had already thought of possible careers for themselves. When she'd asked if they'd like to visit an architect's workplace they and their parents had jumped at the chance. After that another couple of children had shown an interest so here they all were on a Saturday morning heading off to meet Cameron at the station which was to be redeveloped.

Suzi spotted Cameron before he saw them and had a chance to take in his good looks which always seemed to take her by surprise. Her stomach somersaulted, but she was quickly brought back to reality by one of the children asking for the toilet. After Suzi had dealt with that, Cameron proceeded to take them on a tour pointing out the features of the old station which would be incorporated in the new design.

'Now that you've seen what we're working on I'm going to take you to my office and show you the plans and pictures on our computers. But first we're going for a snack and drink in that café over there. My treat.'

The children cheered and Suzi tagged along behind the group as Cameron took charge. The children sat at one table leaving the two adults together at another.

'You're very good with them,' Suzi said.

'I wanted to teach art at secondary school when I was younger. Then a family friend introduced me to architecture and that was it. I was hooked. That's why I didn't hesitate to agree to showing these children round on a Saturday morning.'

'Tom didn't mind?'

'Being at Dorcas's house? Hardly. I think he'd move in if they asked him. As long as Bandit could share his room and sleep on his bed.'

'Miss, Charlie's knocked his hot chocolate over.'

Cameron grinned at Suzi as she leapt

up to fetch some paper towels. She was pleased when he thought to buy a replacement drink for Charlie.

★ ★ ★

'It's my turn now. I want to try out different doors on the building. You've done the windows,' Charlie told his partner as they sat in front of the computer screen at Cameron's office.

'They seem to be enjoying using the programme,' Suzi said

'It's not one we use, a bit too simple, but I thought it would give them some ideas about designing buildings. Working in pairs is good too as they can bounce ideas off each other. What do you think so far?'

Suzi had been studying the way Cameron's golden hair curled into the nape of his neck. 'Lovely,' she said dreamily.

Cameron gave her an odd look then went to help at one of the computers

193

giving her a further opportunity to study him.

Listening to Charlie and his partner chatting easily to each other and exchanging ideas, Suzi drifted off into a daydream. It was Saturday after all and she had missed her lie-in. She stifled a yawn. Then she heard the other pair of children squabbling. It was then she realised that she should have placed Dawn and Lee as far apart from each other as she could. 'Dawn, have you brought a notebook? If so perhaps you'd like to jot down some of the ideas Mr Sanders has outlined. And Lee, you can pair up with Charlie now and find your way around this excellent computer programme.'

Dawn started to protest, but Cameron interjected. 'I'd be pleased if you could write down which designs you like best and why you like them, Dawn. It would help us in the office to know what the consumer thinks. We tend to get a bit above ourselves sometimes and need some sensible person to remind us of the task in hand.'

Suzi watched as Dawn positively preened under Cameron's encouraging words. He'd said just the right thing to deflect a situation which Suzi knew from experience in the classroom could have made the whole morning a disaster. Dawn took a biro from her bag and started writing. After a while she went over to Cameron, and Suzi watched the two of them, heads close together, discussing various points she'd written down.

Lee had calmed down as well now and he and Charlie were discussing the pros and cons of one of the designs in quite a grown up way. It seemed that Cameron, treating the children with respect and deference, had found just the right way to get the best out of them.

Suzi knew without the shadow of a doubt that he would be able to get the best out of her, too — if she gave him the chance . . .

★   ★   ★

Suzi was surprised at the number of parents who turned up on the first evening of the scenery painting. First of all she found out who was capable of more than wielding a paintbrush. Having started the painters off on their tasks she busied herself supervising the construction of the major props and the mechanisms required for the moving and turning of the scenery.

'Now, Cameron, as some of these were your ideas I thought you could supervise this small team of people who are going to construct the clever bits.'

Suzi was kept busy answering questions, opening paint pots and providing both hot and cold drinks. By nine o'clock she was exhausted. She clapped her hands together. 'Okay everyone. I think we've done enough for this evening. If any of you can come back tomorrow that would be fantastic. It's all coming on really well and we should easily finish by the end of the week.'

As the last person left the room Suzi viewed with dismay the mess that had been created. 'Look at all this. These paintbrushes will have to be cleaned and I see someone's spilt paint on the floor. They haven't even put the lids back on the pots. They're messier than the children.'

Cameron took charge. 'You clean the brushes and I'll clear the rest up. We'll have it done in no time.'

When they had finished Cameron took Suzi's hand and led her away from the scenery before turning her back round again. 'Look. You should be pleased. They've done a really good job so far.'

'It's just as I imagined it. I knew it would work using the characteristics of Impressionist paintings.'

'It's brilliant.' Cameron was standing behind her with his hands on her arms. He swung her round and looked into her eyes, before suddenly turning away with, 'I must get back to Tom and relieve Dorcas.'

As he walked away, Suzi felt for Matt's ring. She let out a cry.

'What's wrong, Suzi?' Cameron asked as he rushed back to her.

'I've lost Matt's ring. It could be anywhere.' She burst into inconsolable sobbing and he held her tightly.

'We'll find it. It must be here somewhere. Dorcas told me about Matt so I know how precious the ring is. I promise we'll find it.'

'But all that rubbish we threw out, the newspapers and things. Or it might have gone down the sink when I was washing brushes.' Suzi felt herself going to pieces. She'd well and truly let Matt down losing his precious ring. It was payback time for thinking of Cameron as she had been lately. She slumped against a table. 'It's gone, Cameron.'

'Let's be positive and methodical. We'll start by searching the area where we worked.'

It was getting late as Suzi and Cameron unbundled the rubbish and started to search through it bit by bit.

'We'll never find it,' Suzi said. 'You'd better go home. Dorcas will be wondering where you've got to.'

'I rang her and told her I'm staying here until we find that ring. She agreed I had to.'

'That's kind. Oh, Cameron, I've found it,' Suzi beamed.

'Good, that's very good, but where is it?'

Suzi was holding her cardigan just above the waist. 'I panicked and didn't think. The chain broke and must have slipped down between my shirt and cardigan. Oh, Cameron, thank you very much for being so patient with me, I really don't deserve it.'

'Let's just be pleased you've found it. Would you like me to mend the chain for you when we get home?'

Suzi was touched by Cameron's thoughtfulness after she'd so completely wasted his time. 'That's really lovely, but I don't think so, thank you. I think maybe it's time I put Matt's ring in a box.' Suzi felt she'd reached the point when she should reevaluate a lot of things, including whether she needed to keep Matt's ring around her neck or if it could be put away with his other keepsakes. She'd relied on it heavily for comfort and strength in the past, but she knew she must draw on her own reserves now and have faith in herself.

★   ★   ★

Suzi was happy when Dorcas asked her, Cameron and Tom around for the first free evening after the scenery had been finished. She was even happier that Dorcas had invited them to eat with her, Fred and Olivia. Time with Dorcas and her family was like being at a permanent funfair. Suzi knew Tom would be thrilled to have the chance to play with Bandit. It would be brilliant if Cameron let Tom have a pet of his own, although she knew it was difficult with the house being empty for many hours during the day. She wouldn't interfere now, but given the opportunity, she may suggest it.

Happily, she pulled on a stripy,

strappy top over her slacks. Then she drifted off into her favourite dream about herself and Cameron. Except that the kiss they'd rapturously shared wasn't a dream. It had happened. He must, at the very least, like her. And he'd explained why he'd pulled away. Still, since that evening, he hadn't been anything except distantly polite to her. Perhaps he regretted it. If she got a chance this evening, she'd have a chat with Dorcas to see if she could offer any hints. Suzi envied Dorcas her lovely Fred. Then she reminded herself that she'd had a lovely Matt. Suzi had been convinced that there was only one person anyone could truly, madly, agonizingly fall in love with. Now she wasn't so sure.

* * *

Dorcas came to the door with a huge grin on her face and pulled Tom inside. 'Bandit's waiting for you, love. Go straight through and out the back door.

Get Fred to pour you some lemonade or there's some cola if you prefer.' She didn't invite Suzi or Cameron in and Cameron felt it would be out of place to charge through, especially as Dorcas was standing squarely across the doorway. She appeared to be trying not to laugh as she handed over a small, white envelope before closing the door on them. Over the side gate, Cameron could hear Dorcas padding out into the garden chuckling to herself. Suzi and Cameron looked at each other in amazement.

'What's going on?' asked Suzi, frowning. 'What's that she's given you?'

'We've been set up,' he declared laughing and hugging Suzi in spite of his resolution to keep her at arm's length. 'They're going to keep Tom here until we get back from . . . ' he read from the card inside the envelope, '"Le Gastronomique". Any idea where that is? Hang on, it's that new restaurant in the High Street near the gardens. Very posh.'

Suzi smiled. 'Shall we go, do you think?'

Cameron nodded his head. 'Yes. I'm hungry and we won't get much in there.' He jerked his thumb towards Dorcas's house. 'I'll call a taxi.' He pulled out his mobile phone and pressed the buttons. They didn't have long to wait and were soon on their way.

The restaurant was an oasis of calm. A piano was being played softly at one end of the room and the waiting staff moved almost silently among the tables. They had difficulty making up their minds what to eat as everything sounded delicious.

They sipped their wine and ordered their food. Even though Suzi was smiling across the table at him and inching her hand towards his, he kept his distance. He was finding it increasingly difficult as she was even more appealing sitting so close to him apparently enjoying being with him. From time to time her laughter rang out and he enjoyed the way her hair bounced around her face, her eyes sparkling. When her hand brushed his, it took all his willpower to draw away.

'More wine?' he asked, picking up the bottle and pouring a dribble into her still full wine glass. He replaced the bottle and helped himself to a crusty roll which he played with until it was all crumbs.

'This is delicious,' enthused Suzi, tucking into the fish fillet. 'Is yours okay?'

'Fine.' Cameron felt so stupid. Here he was sitting opposite the woman of his dreams and he was being offhand with her. He struggled through his meal, not really tasting any of it.

When he asked Suzi if she'd like anything more, she said, 'Can I have a pudding, please? I don't suppose I should, but those people over there look as if they're enjoying theirs.' Suzi nodded to a couple who were sharing a large glass plate of a creamy dessert.

'That does look good. One each or

shall we share too?' He was unable to keep up the pretence of indifference with her.

Suzi appeared keen to take up his offer.

'Could we have the same as that couple over there, please?' Cameron asked the waiter.

But when the dessert arrived Suzi looked horrified. 'What's this?' she demanded.

'Coeur a la Crème, Madame.' The waiter hovered by their table. 'It's what you ordered. Would you prefer something else?'

'It's fine, thank you,' Cameron assured the waiter before turning to Suzi. 'Really Suzi what's wrong? It's just a creamy dessert with a raspberry topping.' Cameron was puzzled.

'I couldn't see it properly. I didn't know it was heart shaped.'

Cameron could have kicked himself for ordering a dessert suitable only for lovers, but he hadn't realised. Cameron sensed her unease and was determined to make her feel more comfortable. He took a spoon and dipped it into the dessert. 'It doesn't matter what shape it is. Close your eyes. Now open wide.'

Suzi did as she was told. The mixture of cream, ricotta and yoghurt with the sharpness of the raspberry topping almost made her gasp. 'It's the most luscious taste ever.' She opened her eyes and smiled at Cameron. 'Go on, try some.' Her embarrassment seemed to have been forgotten as she tucked in and encouraged Cameron to do the same. They finished the rich pudding in silence just glancing at each other from time to time.

'I couldn't eat another thing,' puffed Cameron. 'Shall we order coffee?'

Suzi put her hand over his, but he didn't respond. She put her hands in her lap and said, 'That would be nice. It's been a lovely evening, thank you. Although I suppose it's Dorcas we should thank.' Cameron remained silent.

'What's the matter, Cameron?' she

burst out. 'I thought we were getting close after what happened . . . ' Suzi couldn't continue her sentence. She looked upset and didn't seem able to speak.

Cameron knew she was talking about the kiss they'd shared. He hadn't been able to think of much else himself. He simply didn't want anyone to suffer. 'I'm sorry if I gave the wrong impression,' he said quietly, 'but perhaps it would be better if we cool things off a bit. What do you think?' He cringed at what he'd said. How could he do this to her? He watched her face and knew he'd hurt her deeply.

10

Slowly over lazy summer evenings Suzi was absorbed into Cameron and Tom's little unit. She'd been upset for some time after the meal with Cameron, but gradually a relationship of warmth and friendliness had developed. She held herself back from showing her true feelings to him and wasn't sure how much longer she would be able to stay in his home. Practically she thought it would be a good idea to look for somewhere else to live.

'Pimms?' Cameron handed her a tall glass.

She was stirred from her reverie. Cameron and Tom had been working on the garden at weekends and now it was a haven from the busyness of work. Always very peaceful except when they used it as a playground.

'Can we play footie, Dad?' Tom raced

around the garden with the football. He seemed to have a never-ending supply of energy. Suzi was delighted to see him like that.

'Let's have this barbeque first then when our food's gone down maybe Suzi will join us. What do you say?' He turned to her and beamed.

'I could say I've got some preparation to do, but so long as I can go in goal I'll play.' Suzi liked the way she was included by the two of them. Almost as if they were a little family, she thought.

'Yippee! Is the barbeque ready, Dad?' Tom jumped up and down.

'Just about. You nip inside and get any sauces you want and I'll start dishing up.' But when Tom had gone to the kitchen Cameron remained sitting beside Suzi.

'He's a different boy now, don't you think? Really settled and happy. He hardly ever asks after his mother. It's always Mrs Warner this and Suzi that. I don't know how we'd — he'd cope without you.'

'I've been very happy here, too . . . '
She was on the verge of telling him her thoughts about moving.

'Good,' Cameron interrupted, tongs at the ready, 'two sausages?'

Tom chatted away through the meal making the adults laugh. 'Can I give Pinky and Porky some salad?' he asked when he had finished.

The two guinea pigs were in their run happily munching grass.

As Tom hurried off to feed them yet more leaves, Cameron whispered, 'It was a good idea of yours to suggest the guinea pigs after that business with Wynona. They really seem to have helped him. I owe you so much. Perhaps later on I'll be able to repay you in some way.'

'Cameron, I really need to talk to you about my future.' Suzi wanted to unburden herself, but she wasn't looking forward to imparting her news.

'Suzi,' Tom called. 'Come and see. Pinky can open the door to the hutch herself and get into it from the run. Just using her teeth!'

The adults hauled themselves out of their chairs. They admired the guinea pig's cleverness and watched as Tom pushed more things into the cage. 'They like living here,' he declared.

Cameron and Suzi were kept busy by Tom whose energy seemed infinite. But at last the fresh air and food caught up with him and he yawned widely.

'Time for bed, Tommy boy,' called Cameron.

'Five more minutes, Dad, pleeease.' Reluctantly Cameron agreed.

Finally, with Tom tucked up in bed sleeping peacefully, Suzi and Cameron flopped into garden chairs. Suzi closed her eyes and inhaled the evening summer fragrances.

'Are you asleep as well?' Cameron asked quietly. 'I need to know what you're thinking.'

'Everything?' Suzi tried to make light of his question.

'Just about you and me. We make a good team, don't we? You do know that

Tom's got to come first, at least for now. I enjoy spending time with you, but my son's needs are paramount.'

'You've said that, Cameron.' Suzi was a little impatient as they'd been through this many times before. 'We're agreed that Tom must come first.' As Suzi said this she knew it was true. She wouldn't mind being second in Cameron's thoughts, but he didn't seem eager to consider her as anyone other than a friend.

'I just wanted you to know that I do think a lot of you. I wish things could have been different.'

'You said we'd take things slowly and then it was as though you weren't interested in me,' Suzi murmured sadly.

'I'm sorry, I'm not proud of myself. I should have made it clear from the beginning that I just want us to be friends. I can't have the possibility of hurting Tom again.' Cameron shifted his chair so that it was closer to Suzi.

Suzi stood up and glared at him. 'The way you keep going on about Tom being hurt makes me feel that you think I am a bad influence on him. That isn't fair and I can't bear it. If you want to know the truth, I'm thinking of moving away.' Suzi was glad it was out in the open, but she didn't derive any satisfaction from breaking the news so harshly. He scowled back at her and then leapt up and stepped towards her.

'Aren't you happy? I thought you enjoyed our evenings together. I can't tell you how much I look forward to being with you. At work I find myself gazing out of the window thinking of this.' He swept his arm round as though to embrace the garden and Suzi.

Suzi took some deep breaths hoping to calm down a little. She didn't want a bad atmosphere between them, but it was proving very difficult to be with Cameron lately. She had to make him understand, but wasn't sure how to explain. 'It's so hard. I know you know about my husband and I'm glad you haven't overloaded me with sympathy. The thing is Wynona and Matt are still with us; I'm not sure either of us is ready. And caring so much for Tom as we do, I can see why you think us having a relationship might be bad for him. Obviously, if we got together and then it didn't work, the effect on him could be quite damaging.' Suzi felt close to tears.

'That's exactly how I feel, but . . . ' Cameron agreed and reached out for her.

'No, Cameron.' Suzi felt an ache deep in the pit of her stomach. She headed for the patio door.

'Wait, Suzi, please.' Cameron grabbed her shoulders and turned her to look at him. 'I've been so stupid. Why *wouldn't* it work out? We could have been meant for each other. I knew from the moment I saw you that you're special. Wouldn't you regret walking away now, not knowing?' Cameron tilted her chin and gazed into her eyes.

Suzi was in a whirl. She longed for him to kiss her again. However, although she'd fallen in love with him, her sensible side told her that she must remember what Cameron had said about Tom and respect his wishes.

'I'm not sure,' she whispered. She was torn between what she wanted for herself and what Cameron said he wanted. Uncharacteristically, a selfish thought swept through her: why couldn't something in her life work out well for once.

'Neither am I.' Cameron leaned forward and gently brushed her lips with his. 'Perhaps this will help us decide.'

Taken by surprise, Suzi automatically responded to his touch, put her arms round him and pulled him to her. As he responded uncertainty rose in her again. Although she was very attracted to Cameron she didn't want to go through the distress of a commitment which may be snatched away leaving her devastated again. She didn't know how to cope and there was nobody she could ask. It was almost as though Cameron sensed her doubt. He held her close for a while making no demands on her then looping her arm through his he said, 'Don't rush back to your flat. Let's put the guinea pigs to bed then I want to make you something. Please stay a while.'

Suzi knew what she *should* do, but was intrigued to see what Cameron was going to produce. Once the guinea pigs were safely secured in their pen, Cameron insisted she relax in the garden.

It wasn't long before he was back from the kitchen with two glasses on a tray.

'What is it?' Suzi asked intrigued.

'Chocolate milk shake. I think you'll like it.' He handed her a drink and put the tray on the grass.

They clinked glasses and Suzi sipped the drink. 'Mmm, scrumptious,' she said licking the froth from her top lip. 'You're a genius, Cameron Sanders. Now let's see if I can guess the ingredients. Milk, chocolate, coffee, ice-cream.'

'That's enough, no more guessing.

I'm not giving my top secrets away, not even to my favourite lodger.'

Suzi was grateful that once again they were back on an even keel.

'I've some other news, Suzi. I didn't want to say anything while Tom was still about.'

'Oh?' Suzi wondered what it could be. 'Something to do with your work, is it? Your fantastic plans?'

'No, no, nothing like that,' Cameron waved her suggestion aside. 'It's to do with Wynona.'

Suzi stiffened at the mention, once again, of his wife's name. 'What about her?' she asked, more out of politeness than interest. Why did she have to keep coming between them?

'Our decree absolute has come through.' He gave a tight smile. 'I feel rather dejected about the whole business. It's not something to celebrate, but I'm pleased to be able to draw a line under our relationship now. It won't make a lot of difference to Tom in that he won't have any more or any less contact with his mother than if we'd still been married, but I do feel a bit lighter to be free of her legally.'

The news Cameron imparted wasn't what Suzi had been expecting at all and she had no idea how to respond. In a way she felt sorry for Cameron, but she was also pleased that he could now start afresh. 'I hope you'll be able to find the happiness you deserve,' she said.

'Whatever happens in the future, Suzi, I want us to be friends. We've shared quite a lot together.'

Suzi had to admit to herself that they had. At least no one could take those memories away from her. Perhaps a move really was the way forward for her. 'Thank you for a lovely evening, but I really must go now. Night, night Cameron.' She climbed the stairs feeling content for now.

★　★　★

Shortly afterwards Suzi found a leaflet in her letter box with a handwritten message *I'm entering, are you?* It was about an art competition with the theme of summer and the closing date was just a week away. Suzi racked her brains for an idea. She'd like to challenge Cameron in the competition. Then she remembered the lazy summer evening they'd spent recently and thought that if she could capture the atmosphere of that it would be just right. That evening she sorted out her watercolours and brushes and started work. As she was about to bin her third attempt there was a knock on the door. It was Cameron.

'I see you've taken up the challenge. Only a few days to go now.' He studied her latest effort. 'That's good. It's obviously our garden, but you've chosen not to put Tom or me in it.'

'I'm not very good at painting people and I'm not satisfied with this one. I'll keep going until I get it the way I picture it in my mind. What about you? How are you doing?'

'I've framed mine and taken it to the

town hall. I used pastels as it suited what I was trying to achieve. I'm quite pleased with it.'

Suzi thought he was being a bit smug, but that was probably only because he was satisfied with his picture and she didn't have one that was good enough to enter yet.

'I just came to see if you wanted to join us for a bit, but it's clear you're rather busy. How many hours left before the competition closes?' He grinned as he left the flat leaving Suzi more determined than ever to produce her best work.

* * *

Tom tugged at Cameron's arm. 'Come on Dad, where's your picture, and Suzi's?'

'We'll have to look round and find them. There are quite a number, aren't there? And some of them are very good.'

Suzi nodded her agreement. She

would have liked to have a proper look at them, but until Tom had seen their pictures she knew she didn't have a chance.

'Here's Dad's.' Tom pointed excitedly. 'That's me and that's you. Look, there's the guinea pigs' pen.'

'You know I didn't copy your idea, Suzi. I just wanted to remember that lovely evening we had.'

'And you're good at people. They do look like us, don't they Tom?'

'Yeah. Am I in yours too?'

'Sorry, no. Look, here's mine.'

'It's our garden, there's the tree. Have you won? Or Dad?'

'Looking at some of the others I doubt either of us has won or even been placed. But that's not important. We both enjoyed creating them and we also know that our minds sometimes run along similar lines.' Cameron stopped talking to listen to the announcement of the winners and runners up.

'Never mind, Tom, we don't mind at all, do we Suzi?'

'No, but I would like to ask a very big favour. Would it be all right for me to have your picture when the exhibition is finished?'

'Only if I can have yours. I know just where to hang it.'

11

School was increasingly busy throughout the summer term. First of all there were two evening performances and a matinée performance of the musical production. Suzi was kept very busy ensuring the props were in the correct place and that the parents who'd volunteered to help shift the scenery between acts knew what they were doing. On the second evening when Suzi peered round from the side of the stage she spotted Cameron and Tom in the audience. She could barely keep her eyes off them as they were clearly having tremendous fun together. They joined in all the singing, called out as required and laughed at the rather feeble jokes.

At the end Suzi breathed a sigh of relief that none of the scenery had collapsed and that everything had gone smoothly. As she was clearing up Cameron and Tom appeared backstage.

'It was very funny,' Tom said.

'We had a fantastic time and I've never seen scenery quite like it before, not even in the West End.'

Suzi liked it when he teased her.

'Ah, Mr Sanders,' Mr Tanner said. 'We're looking for parents to join us on the younger ones' summer outing. We're going to a zoo. Not the type with big, exotic animals, but one with goats you can get close to and a pet corner. There will be a reptile display so that the children can handle the snakes.'

Cameron shuddered. 'Not my favourite animal.'

'Please, Dad, come.'

'I'd like to, but I'll have to check my work diary and see if I've any meetings that day.'

Tom and Suzi grinned at each other and Tom made a thumbs up sign.

★　★　★

'Are you sure you're okay to come with us, Dorcas?' Suzi asked as everyone gathered in the classroom ready for the outing.

'I'm pregnant, not ill. Anyway, you know Cameron's coming. He'll make sure I don't overdo things. He's as bad as Fred fussing around. I'm really looking forward to seeing the animals.'

'I know we thanked you for the meal at the Le Gastronomique when we picked Tom up, but I just wanted to say again how very generous it was of you and Fred to treat us.'

'It was our pleasure. Fred and me have been through a lot over the years and we've come to realise its people who are important not money. If we can help anyone else find the sort of happiness we enjoy it makes us even happier.'

'That evening was a very nice one, thank you.'

'You and Cameron should go out more often together. I'll have Tom, you know that,' said Dorcas.

'You're very kind and Tom adores coming to see you all.' Suzi didn't confess that Cameron hadn't invited her out and she didn't feel inclined to take the initiative if it meant being rebuffed. Suzi's attention was taken by the eager children.

'There's an adventure playground,' Tom told Olivia excitedly. 'Dad and me looked on the website. There's loads of animals.'

'What? Tigers and lions?'

'Nah, it's not that sort of zoo. It's not for eggsotic animals. There's meerkats, like the one on the telly.'

'Really? Wearing clothes?'

Suzi wondered whether the preparation she'd done with the children over the past few days had been a waste of time. Olivia didn't seem to have remembered anything they'd talked about and Tom had probably learnt more from the internet than her. She wasn't going to let that spoil the day though. The sun was shining and thirty

226

happy children were going to have a wonderful day.

'May I sit next to you, please, Miss?' Cameron asked, after they'd all piled onto the coach.

'Yes, you may.' For today at least they could enjoy themselves. What happened in the future would take care of itself.

'I haven't been on a school outing for years. My last one was a geography trip in the sixth form. We went to Scarborough and Whitby. If I'm honest most of us were more interested in the members of the opposite sex on the trip than anything else.'

Suzi tried to imagine Cameron as a teenager, but it just made her giggle.

'What's up?'

'Nothing, I'm just enjoying myself.'

'The children are very excited, aren't they? I'm not surprised, it's a big day for them.'

'The noise is almost deafening. If they don't quieten down soon Mr Tanner will be having a word,' Suzi said.

'Does he lead the singing?'

'We thought you'd do that having heard you during the musical.'

'I just got carried away. I'm a very happy man. Haven't you heard me singing round the house?'

Suzi laughed. 'Tom's happy too. Putting him first was exactly the right thing to do. You're a wonderful dad.'

'And you're just wonderful.'

Suzi didn't know what to say. Their relationship was good now and she wished she had the willpower to stay and enjoy it, but her feelings for Cameron were all consuming. It wouldn't be right to stay.

'What's wrong, Suzi?' Cameron asked as he took her hand and gently squeezed it.

'Nothing at all. Today's going to be perfect. One of those days we remember forever.'

★ ★ ★

'I've got guinea pigs at home,' Tom told some of his friends as they were sitting on the grass eating their picnic.

'I've got a dog,' one said.

'I've got a tiger,' said Olivia.

'No you haven't, you've got a Bandit,' Tom told her.

'I'm getting a tiger for Christmas,' she insisted.

'No, you're not, you're getting a baby.'

'I hope I have it before Christmas.' Dorcas laughed. 'What did you think of the snakes, Cameron?'

'Horrible things,' he said shivering. 'I don't know how the children could bear to have them draped round their necks. Give me a fluffy rabbit or guinea pig any day. What's on the agenda for the afternoon?'

Suzi had a think. 'They've got to finish off their worksheets, then there's a trail where they follow clues. Then the rest of the afternoon is going to be spent in the adventure playground followed by a quick visit to the shop for them to spend their pocket money if they want to. Let's hope they'll all be so tired we'll have a quiet trip home.'

'You mean as in no singing? Spoil-sport,' grinned Cameron.

Suzi delegated a couple of parents and some children to clear up the rubbish and put it in the bins provided and the afternoon progressed well. The period after lunch was devoted to the worksheets which the children seemed to enjoy. Suzi hoped it would make them think a bit more widely about the world around them.

The trail wasn't quite as she'd envisaged, however, with one of the children falling into a bunch of stinging nettles. Dorcas took over then and rubbed the little girl's legs with dock leaves before taking her back to the picnic area and dabbing on calamine lotion.

'I'm glad Dorcas can have a rest,' murmured Suzi to Cameron. 'She puts more than a hundred per cent of herself into everything she does.'

'Olivia looks a bit put out, though,' observed Cameron. 'I wonder if she's a bit jealous. It must be difficult having to share your mother with other children all the time. I wonder how she'll react when the little baby comes along.'

'I suppose that will be a bit different as the baby will sort of belong to Olivia as well,' said Suzi. She called out, 'Olivia, why don't you come and walk with me? You can help me work out which way we should be going.'

'Don't want to,' sulked Olivia.

'Anyway, Olivia's walking with me,' protested Tom.

Suzi could see she was fighting a losing battle and shrugged her shoulders at Cameron.

The group continued on the trail and in a short while had arrived back where they'd started with a collection of grasses, leaves and other interesting things they'd picked up on the way.

'Well done, everyone. Now you can take a little time to draw the things you've collected.' She handed out pencils and papers. 'And then we can go to the adventure playground.'

With the children clambering over the equipment, Suzi took time to speak to Dorcas. 'Thanks for taking charge of Emily. She seems all right now.'

'Olivia's got a face on her, though,' said Dorcas. 'She's been a bit moody lately. I think she was looking forward to Fred coming, pity he was called into work at the last minute. Still, can't be helped. You and Cameron seem to have spent a lot of time together. I noticed he made a beeline to sit next to you on the coach.'

'He's been quite helpful. Did you see him with a little group of children when we got back from the trail? I thought they might find it difficult to draw those leaves, but he got them to trace the outlines and then colour them in.' She looked at her watch. 'Another quarter of an hour and then I suppose we'd better let them go into the gift shop. I expect they only allow a few at a time, so the ones outside will have to be patient.'

'Cameron and I will fix up some sort

of game for them. Don't worry, Suzi.'

'I'll get some of the other parents involved, Dorcas. You're doing far too much.'

Tom and Olivia were in the second group of children to visit the shop. They'd been whispering together and Suzi guessed they were deciding what to buy. After the requisite ten minutes had elapsed, Suzi called to them all, 'Time's up. Everyone outside now, please and let the others come in.'

The children scooted out of the shop and across to a grassy area where Cameron and the other parents were playing an elaborate game of I-spy. As Suzi was ushering the next group into the shop, she caught sight of Olivia stuffing something into her little backpack. Intrigued, she went over to her. 'What did you buy, Olivia? May I see?'

'No,' replied the little girl, squirming away. 'It's a secret.'

At that moment, Cameron stood up and wandered over. 'Is everything all right?'

'Of course,' said Suzi. 'I just wondered what the children had bought from the shop, that's all.' It was being blown up out of all proportion and it looked as if Olivia was going to have a tantrum. It was lucky that Dorcas was around, except she wasn't now as Suzi saw her disappearing towards the ladies' room.

'Why don't you join in the game with Mr Sanders, Olivia? I'm going back to the shop.'

Olivia turned pale and her teeth started chattering. 'I only did it for the baby,' she said, making no sense at all to Suzi or Cameron.

'Did what?' asked Suzi kneeling down to be on a level with Olivia who was getting more and more upset.

'The tiger is for Mummy's baby. Tom said she'd like one,' stammered Olivia, taking the stuffed toy out of her bag and pushing it towards Suzi.

'Well that was very kind,' replied Suzi carefully. Whatever had happened to make Olivia this upset?

'It was too much money.'

Suzi glanced up at Cameron and they understood what had transpired. 'So you took it and didn't pay the money to the lady in the shop. Is that right?'

Olivia nodded. 'Will they send me to prison?'

'Certainly not,' said Cameron, taking charge. 'Look, I tell you what, if you promise to tell your mummy exactly what happened then I'll take the toy back to the shop and explain it to them.'

Olivia hiccoughed and nodded her head, the colour returning to her cheeks.

'Hello, love,' sang out Dorcas returning to the group. 'Are you having a lovely time?'

'I want to go home,' stated Olivia. 'And Tom's dad said I had to tell you something.'

'Okay then, come over here and let me take the weight off my feet. Then I can have a nice cosy chat with my favourite daughter.' She plonked a kiss on Olivia's cheek and the two went off hand in hand.

'Let's wait a minute and see what happens,' said Cameron, leaning against the wall of the gift shop, holding the stuffed toy behind him.

After a little while, Suzi saw Olivia running over towards them. 'Did you take the tiger back?' she asked Cameron.

'Not yet,' he said, pulling it out from behind his back.

Olivia snatched it and ran into the shop. Suzi followed; Olivia was her responsibility as well as Dorcas's.

Breathlessly Olivia said to the woman behind the counter, 'I didn't have enough money for this. I'm sorry.' Then she handed over the toy.

'Thank you for telling me,' said the assistant. 'Put it back with the others would you, please?' Then she turned to serve a customer who wanted to buy a postcard of the pets' corner. The matter appeared to be closed.

From then on, Suzi kept a close eye on Olivia. It had been a hard lesson for her. Looking at Dorcas's troubled face when she thought no one could see, gave Suzi another insight into the difficulty of parenting. Suzi saw Tom go over to Olivia and speak to her. Olivia was gesturing towards the shop and towards her mum. Tom put his arm around Olivia and led her away from the group of children. They sat under a tree and immersed themselves in deep conversation. After a while they smiled at each other and made some sort of secret sign with their hands: a cross between a thumbs up and a high five. Suzi was fascinated. It appeared that they'd come to some sort of conclusion which suited them both and they were friends. If only things could be sorted out as amicably and satisfactorily between adults.

'Are we going home soon, Mrs Warner?' asked Emily, rubbing her legs. 'I want my mum.'

'Do your legs still hurt?' asked Suzi, bending down to inspect them. There was no sign of any rash now.

'Not really,' admitted Emily, 'but I'd like to see my mum.'

Suzi looked at her watch. 'You're quite right, Emily. Thank you for reminding me of the time. Would you like to be first in the line?' The expression on the little girl's face told Suzi she'd said the right thing.

After counting the children and adults back onto the coach, Suzi said to Cameron, 'Remind me never to suggest a day out again as long as I'm in charge of a class of six year olds!'

Cameron chuckled and stood aside to let Suzi board the vehicle which would take them all home. There was no way Suzi could divert his attention and he soon had the children singing on the return journey. Even Mr Tanner joined in and manfully, although a little off key and a beat behind everyone else, warbled his way through *In a cottage in a wood*.

Suzi leaned her head against the window pane and reflected that Cameron was a wise man. If he hadn't waited to see what would transpire between Dorcas and her daughter, the whole situation regarding the toy might have escalated. If it was possible, he had gone up in her estimation quite a few notches.

12

It must have been the middle of the night when a commotion woke Suzi a few days later and she sat up in bed wondering what was going on. Raised voices in the house had her bumping around in the darkened bedroom trying to wake up properly. From her small landing, she could make out a woman's strident voice and Cameron, imploring her to keep her voice down. The American accent gave the game away as to who Cameron was entertaining.

Suzi's heart plummeted as she thought over her rollercoaster emotional journey since Cameron had arrived in her life. She really thought that after the barbeque he did think a lot of her. He'd told her that he'd fallen out of love with Wynona and was finally divorced, yet in no time at all here they were back together. She'd thought he'd meant what he said, but her judgement of him must have been mistaken.

At least Suzi couldn't hear Tom's little voice among the conversation; hopefully he was fast asleep. Just a couple of weeks to the summer break and Suzi could move out of this house for good. She'd visit her parents and enjoy being pampered by them. Judging by her last attempt to find accommodation, it wasn't going to be easy to find somewhere near the school. Unless — unless she finished working at the school and found another job as well. A good, clean break. Even if she just moved house, she'd still come into contact with Cameron at school functions and Tom would be a daily reminder of the family she'd shared for a brief time. She'd miss the school and Dorcas and her family, even Mr Tanner, but she was sure she'd get a good reference from him. Having decided that was her only course of action, Suzi crept back to the comfort of her bed and tried to doze.

Suzi attempted to tiptoe unnoticed out of the house early in the morning. Just as she was creeping downstairs, Wynona appeared from Cameron's bedroom. 'Well, look who it is. Cameron can't stop talking about you. He thinks you're a perfect tenant.'

'Not for much longer,' Suzi snapped, hurrying down the next flight of stairs. She found it hard to believe that Cameron had taken Wynona back again after all that he'd said about her. Really she felt like hiding herself away, but she had to face her responsibilities.

She immersed herself in her teaching, trying not to let Tom remind her of his father. But it was difficult. Her attention kept wandering and the children grew restless. They were all pleased when the lunch break arrived. Suzi couldn't bear to be closed in the staff room with the other teachers today, so took a walk around the block to see if it could clear her head. How many more days could she endure the agony she was suffering?

By the afternoon Suzi had decided that a practice for sports day out in the fresh air was just what she and her class needed. It was the perfect day for running around and letting off steam. As she assembled a group of children for the first race a familiar figure walked towards her. 'Can I help you, Mr Sanders? We're a bit busy here as you can see. Would you like a word with Mr Tanner?'

'No,' said Cameron quietly. 'What I want is a word with *you*.'

The children were growing restless again and Mr Tanner's look wasn't approving. Suzi suggested that Cameron watch from the sidelines with Mr Tanner until she was free. She tried to carry on as normal getting her class to go through their paces for the events they'd chosen to take part in, but she was very aware that Cameron was following her every move. She was intrigued that he wanted to talk to her, but she was still angry and upset about bumping into Wynona that morning.

★ ★ ★

Cameron had watched as Suzi organised the children into teams, encouraged the reluctant runners and praised everyone. He longed for her tenderness after the latest fracas with Wynona.

As he thought of his ex-wife, anger seethed just below the surface. She'd promised to keep out of their way until she returned to America. Yet she had to descend on Cameron in the middle of the night just to tell him that Dmitri had dumped her. She hadn't said those words, of course, but that's what it amounted to. Another, younger woman had taken Wynona's place, was Cameron's guess. But along with Dmitri, this other woman had also taken Wynona's promised promotion and its attendant money and kudos. Cameron hadn't been remotely interested in the circumstances, but it had always been difficult to stop Wynona once she got into her stride. From experience, he had known he'd have to hear her out, which is what he did. He'd also allowed her to stay, which had been a big mistake because she saw Tom before he went off to school. The little chap had been confused which was why Cameron had come to the school. Thank goodness Suzi hadn't been disturbed during the night by Wynona's presence.

Cameron hardly noticed the races, but he clapped automatically when Mr Tanner did and called encouragement to the children. All he wanted was for the afternoon to be over and Suzi and Tom safely at home with him. To his relief the children were sent indoors for a drink and the equipment was being packed up by a couple of willing helpers. He approached Suzi and took a net of balls from her, dangling it from one hand.

★   ★   ★

'What was it you wanted?' Suzi asked.

'I wanted to explain,' Cameron began. 'Wynona came yesterday and saw Tom this morning and I'm afraid it might have unsettled him.'

Suzi had no wish to get involved in a conversation featuring Wynona, so she hurried to get away from him, unintentionally banging against the net Cameron was carrying. The balls spilled out and bounced away. When she reached the school doorway, she glanced behind to see Cameron chasing the balls and returning them to their net.

At no time during their brief conversation did Cameron say that he hoped she, Suzi, had not been disturbed by Wynona's presence. But perhaps his ex-wife hadn't seen fit to tell him that the two had met on the stairs earlier on. She despaired of the situation. It was becoming foolish. Cameron would have to sort out the situation with Wynona and lay down some rules for Tom's sake. She tried not to think about it anymore; it had nothing to do with her.

Back in the classroom Suzi congratulated the children for doing so well during their sports practice and then it was time for them to go home. Tom had already gone with Cameron, and Suzi was relieved she didn't have to face him again — at least until she returned home.

When all the children had been collected, Suzi went to the staff cloakroom and splashed her face with cold water. From her bag she took a brush and untangled her hair. Her mind was made up now and she'd carry out her plan before she could change her mind.

Steeling herself to tell him that she was handing in her resignation, Suzi gave Mr Tanner's office door a brief knock before opening it. Seeing he was on the phone, she smiled an apology and left. Perhaps it would be better to wait until a day when she was more composed. So much for her positive attitude. Was nothing going to work out right for her? She couldn't even hand in her resignation properly.

Not wanting to return to the flat and risk bumping into Cameron until it was absolutely necessary, and avoiding Dorcas's buzzing household, Suzi decided a bit of shopping would take her mind off her current situation.

★ ★ ★

'Goodness, Suzi, I've never seen you in lime green before,' Dorcas said to her friend the following afternoon when she collected the children.

'Ghastly isn't it? It's put me in a bad mood all day. I'm going to put it in the charity bag as soon as I've washed it. I had a disastrous shopping trip yesterday after school, my mind just wasn't on it.'

Dorcas looked at her kindly. 'Come on, Suzi, you look as though you need a sympathetic shoulder.'

'And?' Suzi could tell there was something more.

'Well, I would like to know what's

been going on. What with Cameron coming in to school yesterday and taking Tom home for no apparent reason. When he rang to tell me, he sounded very agitated. I've never known him be like that before.' Dorcas raised her eyebrows questioningly at Suzi. 'I'm just guessing it's something to do with you, am I right?'

'I don't know if I want to talk about it and anyway I have masses of work to do.' She indicated the two piles of exercise books on her desk.

'Why not do a bit then come round? It'll give me a chance to get some jobs done. I'll give the kids a drink and snack before you come so we can have some peace and quiet — we can but hope.' Dorcas wasn't taking no for an answer and walked out of the classroom door before Suzi could reply.

Suzi was soon absorbed in her work. It was only her mobile ringing that reminded her she was meant to be at Dorcas's by now.

'I'm waiting and I'm very persistent,'

Dorcas trilled down the phone. 'I've even put the kettle on.'

Suzi couldn't help laughing and quickly made her way to Dorcas's house. As soon as she walked in she relaxed.

'Now, you sit here while I pour the tea,' Dorcas insisted before abruptly rubbing her eyes and sitting down herself.

'What is it?' Suzi was already at her side, worried about her paleness. 'What's wrong with your eyes?'

'My vision's a bit blurred, that's all.'

'Shall I call Fred at work? Perhaps he should take you to see the doctor.'

'No, no, let's not worry him, I'll be fine, honestly. Let me sit here quietly for a minute.'

'Here, drink your tea,' Suzi said, handing over a mug. She was worried. 'Has this happened before?'

Dorcas pulled a wry face. 'A couple of times. But I didn't tell Fred, I didn't want to worry him. He's got a lot going on at work so me being ill is the last thing he needs. Feeling unwell at times is just one of those things you have to put up with when you're pregnant.'

'I'm not so sure. I don't know much about it, but I do think tomorrow you'd better make an appointment to see your doctor just to be checked over.'

'Okay, nurse Suzi, whatever you say. Anyway, I feel much better already. Now why don't you tell me what's been going on in the Sanders' household. Or was it simply that Cameron was missing you and had to see you! I can't understand why he went to school to watch a P.E. lesson.'

'It was nothing to do with him missing me. Wynona turned up and stayed the night. Can you believe it? I met her the following morning.'

'What's so wrong in that?' asked Dorcas looking puzzled. 'Why shouldn't she stay at the house? Like her or loathe her, she's Tom's mum after all.'

Suzi felt silly; of course Wynona could stay at the house and anyone else Cameron wanted to be there. Things were getting on top of her in a big way now and she knew she had to get away.

'What about little Tom? What effect will this have on him, her dropping in and out of his life?' asked Dorcas.

'Yes, poor lad. I don't suppose I'll help him much either. I may be going to look for a new job elsewhere.'

'What? Where are you going? You can't do that. All those children losing you. And what does Mr Tanner say? He speaks very highly of you. And what about *me*? You're my friend and I need you especially with the new baby,' complained Dorcas.

'Don't be so gloomy, Dorcas. Maybe I won't go far. You and Fred can come and visit with Olivia and the new baby. I did *try* to make a new start here, but it hasn't worked out. Perhaps I should go back to my home town where I know a few people. I've been coming to terms with Matt's death at last and I think now I would be all right going to places we went to together and meeting up with mutual friends. I didn't believe people when they told me time heals, but in a way it does. I still have my memories of Matt, but I can think of him now without crying. I feel a lot stronger except for this problem with Cameron, although he helped me get over Matt.' She couldn't stop the tears welling. 'He's confusing me so much.'

'Just wait 'til I see him. I'll give him a good telling off. I thought he was a decent bloke, I'm not usually wrong. Fred will be furious — he's very fond of you.'

'That sounds like a key in the front door, he must be home. I'll be on my way. Please promise me you'll tell him about your blurred vision and make that appointment with the doctor.'

'Yes, Miss, I promise.'

★　★　★

The following day, Fred phoned the school notifying Suzi that Dorcas had been admitted to hospital.

'How is she?' Suzi burst out.

'We're not sure. They're keeping her in for a few days to see what's going on. She has high blood pressure and doesn't feel at all well.'

'Oh, Fred, what a worry for you, but she's in the best place. I'm sure she'll be well looked after.'

'You're probably right. There is something I need to ask you. It's a big favour. I'd really like to spend as much time as possible at the hospital as you can understand. I wondered if you'd be willing to look after Olivia and Bandit and stay with us. Just until Dorcas is home again.' Fred sounded desperate.

'I'm very happy to stay for as long as I'm needed. Don't worry about a thing at home. You spend as much time as you like with Dorcas. Is the spare key hidden in the usual place?'

She took Olivia and Tom to Dorcas's house at the end of the school day. Tom was happy as he'd promised Bandit a game of hide and seek in the garden. But Olivia was distressed that her mother had not arrived to collect her as usual.

Suzi related the situation as straightforwardly as she could. Olivia clung to her skirt and Suzi bent down and drew her into her arms. 'Mum will soon be home, Olivia. Try not to worry about her. The doctors and nurses will make her well. Your dad is going to spend time with her and he'll let us know how she's getting along. I'm sure she'd like it if you drew a picture for her or made her a get well card.'

At the mention of being able to do something for her mum, Olivia brightened. 'I can draw Bandit,' she said. 'That'll cheer her up, won't it?'

'I'm sure it will,' replied Suzi, amazed at the resilience of children, even though she'd witnessed it often in the classroom.

With Tom and Bandit racing around the garden and Olivia at work designing her mum's card, Suzi made herself some tea and ferreted around the cupboards and fridge wondering what to make Olivia and herself for supper. She didn't know if Fred would be home to eat or not, but decided to make enough for him as well just in case. Although Suzi was desperately sorry that Dorcas was in hospital, she was pleased that she had been asked to look after Olivia and Bandit; it was just the change of scene she needed at the moment.

It wasn't long before Cameron popped his head round the kitchen door with a cheery, 'Hi there, Dorcas.' His face fell. 'Suzi? What's going on?'

Suzi explained once again in an unemotional manner, then added, 'I'm going to have to come back to your house now to collect my stuff. We'll have to take Olivia with us, too. I'll only need a few overnight things.'

Cameron grasped Suzi's arm. 'I hope you won't be staying away long. We have to talk. I've more things to tell you.'

'Can't you tell me now?' She made

256

sure Tom and Bandit were still in the garden and Olivia was out of earshot before sitting at the table ready to listen to whatever Cameron had to say.

'Wynona invited herself to the house. She was in one of her moods and wouldn't be dissuaded from staying. I didn't want her around for many reasons, but the main one was in case she upset Tom once more.'

'I was worried she'd wake Tom up,' said Suzi, innocently letting slip the fact that she'd been aware of Wynona's presence.

'So you *did* hear her,' sighed Cameron. 'And that's why you were a bit off with me. Is that it?' When Suzi didn't reply, he continued, 'I suppose I can't blame you for that.'

Suzi couldn't afford to get side-tracked now with Cameron. She stood up and was about to call Tom in from the garden when Olivia came into the kitchen.

'I've made this,' she said, holding out a picture of a dog with its red tongue lolling out of its mouth. 'Can you help me write on it, Mrs Warner?'

By the time Suzi had finished lending Olivia a hand with forming the letters, Cameron and Tom had left.

13

Suzi was overjoyed when Fred asked her to visit Dorcas a couple of days later. She'd missed her friend and was looking forward to seeing her again. She also wanted to reassure her that she was looking after her little family and there was nothing to worry about.

Dorcas was back to her normal ebullient self as she waved Suzi into the ward. 'Nurse,' Dorcas called, after enveloping Suzi in a hug. 'My visitor's going to take me outside. I suppose I'll need a wheelchair for that?'

Once outside, Dorcas sniffed the air. 'I'll be glad to get back home. They're very nice to me, but I don't want to stay much longer. How's my little Olivia? I think I shouldn't spread myself so thinly. Poor little kid always seems to have to share me. After that incident at the zoo we've got into a routine of having a special time together, just the two of us. It's really good that since I've been in this place she's been having a special time with Fred each evening. Are you sure she's all right?'

'She's great,' Suzi assured her. 'And Fred's fine too.'

'Ah, I know my Fred. He's putting on a brave face, but I know he's worried to death. I wish I could have coped better and not been brought into here in the first place.'

'It's nothing to do with being able to cope. You couldn't have done anything to prevent it. As for your Fred, he's one in a million — well probably two or three million,' smiled Suzi. She parked the wheelchair by the rose bushes and sat on a low wall. 'You're both very lucky to have each other. A soulmate. That's what I wanted. And I had it — with Matt.'

Dorcas reached for Suzi's hand and squeezed it. 'You can learn to love again,' she told her. 'It's like riding a bike.' She fidgeted in the wheelchair. 'Tell me it's none of my business if you like, but are you still angry with Cameron?'

Suzi leant towards Dorcas and told her about the latest situation with her and Cameron.

'So, she invited herself and he couldn't do much about it once she'd gone upstairs and fallen asleep. He didn't want her there,' Suzi explained.

'I'm so pleased,' squealed Dorcas, putting her hands up to hug Suzi. 'I felt sure he wasn't a bad apple.' Dorcas gave Suzi a searching look. 'What is it, Suzi? You don't seem very happy. It's pretty straightforward to me. Cameron and Wynona are divorced, he doesn't care for her one bit and he likes you. Unless there is something you're not telling me. Isn't it enough for now to know he doesn't love Wynona?'

'It's not that. I just feel so, well, I think guilty is the word. Sometimes I feel all right about moving on and sometimes I feel awful about it. I don't want to be unfaithful to Matt. We were so close.'

'That's understandable. But I think one of the difficulties is that it will be very hard for anyone to match up to Matt in your mind. From what you've told me he was a fantastic, brave, fearless, man.'

'The other problem is I don't know how to handle commitment, Dorcas; I don't want to fall headlong in love only to be hurt again. I feel I may be being very selfish in thinking like that.' Suzi was lost for a moment in her own thoughts.

Dorcas patted her hand and waited quietly.

'I don't know what you're going to think, but I've had a lot of dreams, especially since meeting Cameron. Matt figures in them all. It's as though he's still around and I wonder what he wants.' She brushed at her eyes. 'Do you think I'm being silly?'

'No, I don't, but I tell you what, I think Matt *is* still around and he's keeping an eye on you. I don't pretend to know about the spirit world or whatever you may call it, but I'm sure that they help us poor mortals.' She let out a ripple of laughter. 'We need it, don't we? If you're asking for my advice, I'd say that Matt has seen that you can be happy with Cameron and he's come to say that he approves. I think he may have come to say goodbye and wish you well. That's what you'd do for him if the roles were reversed, wouldn't you?'

'Oh, yes,' Suzi whispered. 'Definitely.'

'That part of your life is over; it has no power to hurt you anymore.' Dorcas grasped Suzi's hand and brought it to her soft cheek before grinning up at her in her typically cheery way. 'I suppose I'd better be getting back into that ward before they send out a search party. Did Fred send any chocolates?'

★   ★   ★

Dorcas was discharged at the end of the week, so Suzi collected her belongings together and went back to her flat.

'Hi there,' Cameron called up the stairs, 'fancy a cuppa? I've got the kettle on. It's good to have you back home.' He smiled at her.

A grin crossed Suzi's face. Home? Did he think she regarded his house as her home? She found the thought quite warming.

'Tom's gone to a friend's house for the weekend. We could have a day out together tomorrow. What do you say? What would you like to do?'

Suzi wasn't expecting this. She'd love to spend time with Cameron. 'Great. I'd like that. I don't mind what we do.'

'I thought you were going to turn me down,' admitted Cameron. 'We could go to the park. It's going to be sunny.'

'What time were you thinking of?' Suzi asked as she drained her coffee.

'Whenever you're ready. Just let me know and we'll take things as they come, shall we?'

Suzi had seen Cameron like this before. He was enthusiastic and lively as they walked in the park. She recognised once again that when he didn't have Tom with him he was much more relaxed. He took his parenting so seriously and Suzi admired him for it. It was such a shame that he couldn't be like this more often. A football came rolling along in front of them and Cameron chased it along the path doing some nifty footwork before returning it to the group of lads. The day turned warm and he took off his sweater, hanging it around his shoulders.

'Ice cream?' he asked.

'Please,' returned Suzi. 'What shall we have?' She liked the change in him. 'I think I'd like a 99.'

'Two 99s, please,' he ordered from the ice cream vendor. 'Here, it's dripping already.'

Suzi licked at the cone, giggling when Cameron patted away a blob on her nose. 'This reminds me of being at the seaside when I was a kid,' she said. 'Ice cream, candy floss, toffee apples.'

'I love it when you're like that,' he

said, popping the last piece of cone into his mouth.

'Like what?'

'When you enthuse about something, when you're so full of . . . ' Cameron didn't finish his sentence. He pulled Suzi towards him and put his arms around her, stroking her hair and gently kissing the top of her head. Suzi turned her face up towards his and their lips tenderly met. As far as she was concerned, she'd happily have stayed like that for ever. How could she have doubted that Cameron cared for her? Perhaps everything would be all right for the two of them if their relationship developed. A small part of her could envisage an exquisite future with Cameron, but a larger part whispered to her that there were obstacles in their path to happiness.

'Shall we have a meal together when we get back? I don't mean for either of us to cook. Let's be lazy and get a take-away. We could watch a DVD,' said

Cameron, apparently oblivious to Suzi's unease.

'That sounds lovely,' she said.

★ ★ ★

'That was really tasty,' stated Suzi, declining a second helping of chow mein. It felt right to be with Cameron. If nothing else they had a wonderful friendship. She should be satisfied with that.

'You choose the film,' said Cameron. 'I'm going to finish these prawns.'

Suzi sorted through a pile of DVDs, discarding any romantic ones as they must have been Wynona's; she couldn't envisage Cameron or Tom buying them. She handed over a DVD to Cameron.

'Are you sure?' he asked, his eyebrows raised.

'You don't mind, do you?' asked Suzi, smiling.

'I've only watched it a million times before, but okay if that's what you want, 101 Dalmatians it is, then.'

They sat beside each other on the settee, Cameron's arm around Suzi's shoulders. She rested her head against him and they relaxed together.

★   ★   ★

When the film had finished and Cameron had cleared the plates away, she excused herself and went upstairs. She'd spent a happy day in the presence of the man she'd grown to love, but it seemed impossible that they would ever be able to be anything more than friends. She was prepared to admit to herself that, although she would never forget Matt and the time they spent together, she was gradually getting used to him no longer being around. She could also see that one day, even if it wasn't now with Cameron, she could be in a serious relationship with someone other than Matt. It was a possibility which Cameron had enabled her to envisage.

She fetched the mementoes from

the wardrobe. After glancing quickly through the cuttings, she took the ring from the box and held it briefly before putting it back. Then she re-tied the ribbon round the cuttings. She put the things away, hoping that she could move forward with her life without relying on those physical reminders of Matt's which had kept her going since his death. Maybe she wouldn't feel the need to open the box again.

★   ★   ★

Cameron had begged her to join him for a picnic the following day. Suzi heard the front door slam early in the morning and guessed that he'd gone to get some food for the outing. She took care choosing what to wear and eventually settled on a floral print ruffle dress with full blown, hot pink roses on a cream background. When she reached the bottom of the stairs, Cameron was already in the hall waiting.

'Wow, you look sensational. I don't

think I should take you out anywhere, you'll have a stream of admirers after you.'

'Flatterer!' beamed Suzi, pleased that she'd taken the trouble to look extra good, and happy that he had at least noticed. 'You don't look too bad yourself.' He was wearing slim fit cotton twill chinos in a light grey, topped with a Breton striped cotton sweater. On his feet he sported grey and blue panelled boat shoes. 'Maybe you shouldn't go out either.'

'I've got it all arranged and I've just had another brilliant idea. Let's take our painting things. If we go down to the river there will be some lovely views. I'll meet you back here in ten minutes.' Without waiting for a reply he was gone. Suzi went back upstairs and put together a bag with all her watercolour paints and brushes. It would be a good way to spend the day — doing something they both enjoyed.

Once again Cameron was full of

enthusiasm as they drove to the agreed beauty spot. The journey didn't take long and Suzi almost wished for longer just to chat and sit close to him. Once parked, Cameron led her across a stile and through a meadow. They had quite an array of luggage between them what with the hamper of food and their painting equipment. When they reached the river the sun was shining and the only sounds were birdsong and an occasional boat chugging past. There wasn't another person in sight, not even a fisherman.

'It's beautiful here.' Suzi settled on the rug they'd spread out on the bank under a tree. She watched lazily as he set up an easel and clipped paper to it. 'You use that,' she called. 'I think I'll just sit here and sketch with my block and pencils.'

'We can change over later if you like.' He prised open a box of watercolours and looked around him. 'Now, what shall I paint?'

'How about the bull that's coming up

behind you?' asked Suzi.

'I'm not falling for that,' laughed Cameron. 'I think I might try and do something for next year's competition. You'll enter again won't you?' He immersed himself in his painting.

Suzi ignored his remark as she wouldn't be around next year to enter. She had made several sketches, but as usual was never quite satisfied with the results. 'Are you hungry yet?' she asked, stretching out and tossing her sketch pad onto the rug.

'Starving. Must be the fresh air. I'm pleased with my painting. It might be a winner. Give me a couple of minutes and I'll lay the food out.'

But Suzi already had the lid off the hamper and was arranging things on the colourful plastic plates Cameron had packed. He dragged himself away from his picture and washed his hands in the river.

'Goodness,' exclaimed Suzi, 'did you buy the entire supermarket? What a spread.'

'This might be a bit warm now,' Cameron said picking up a bottle and popping the cork. He poured the pink champagne into plastic flutes and handed one to Suzi. 'To us,' he said raising his glass.

Without attempting to fill plates for themselves, they chose and fed each other titbits.

'These olives are delicious,' exclaimed Suzi, holding one to Cameron's mouth for him to taste.

'The cheese is really ripe. Try some.' Cameron speared a morsel on the end of a fork and held it to Suzi's lips. Then he took a slice of walnut bread and loaded it with mozzarella and succulent fresh dates. After cutting the slice in half, he held a piece out to Suzi. They each took a bite and chewed appreciatively.

When Suzi lifted her glass to her mouth, Cameron mirrored her, his eyes not moving away until their glasses were empty. Then he leant over and said, 'Look at the dessert.' He proudly took the lid off a container. 'Try one of these.'

'They're rather special.' Suzi singled out a large pink meringue bursting with cream, which was already melting. She separated the two halves and held one out to Cameron. As he lifted it to his mouth, the confection collapsed and crumbled into pieces. The crumbs he brushed from his sweater scattered over the rug.

'I'm making a right mess of this.'

'Here, have mine,' offered Suzi.

'I think I'd better just stick to strawberries, thanks.' He heaped some up on a shortbread biscuit and took a bite. 'We ought to do this more often.'

After lunch Suzi lay on the rug gazing at the clouds scudding across the sky. Cameron was sketching.

'There, finished,' he said handing her the block.

It was a drawing of her face, perfectly executed. 'You really are very talented, Cameron.'

'And you Suzi Warner are the

loveliest woman I've ever met.' He joined her on the rug and outlined her face with his fingers. Then he took her hand and brought it to his lips. They lay silently together in the dappling sunshine.

* * *

The previous day had been brilliant. When they'd collected Tom and driven home, Cameron had insisted that the portrait he'd done of her be exhibited with his others along the walls going up the stairs alongside the one he'd exchanged with her after the competition. Now Suzi came down to earth with a bang. Here goes, she thought, perched on the edge of the chair opposite Mr Tanner. 'I've been thinking about my future. I'd like to talk over the possibility of leaving my job.' She didn't know where she found the strength to say the words after everything had seemed so right with Cameron by the river.

Mr Tanner looked stunned. 'Really? I'm gobsmacked as the children say. I'm not prepared to lose a valuable member of staff just like that. Would you mind telling me why?'

'Personal reasons. I'm not saying any more.'

'Mmm. I think I have an inkling. It's that Cameron Sanders. He seems a charming chap, but you can never tell. Bit of a ladies man, is he? Bit of a rogue? Let you down?'

'No, it's not like that.' Suzi didn't want to talk about Cameron.

'Maybe the best thing to do would be to move out of his flat and live elsewhere. Then you could continue quite happily here at school. The other thing is, I don't know when you had in mind, but I do require a certain length of notice. For instance, you can't just go at the end of term.'

Suzi felt very stupid. Of course Mr Tanner would need time to find a replacement, but also she now didn't know if she was absolutely sure she wanted to leave. It had been so lovely being with Cameron and the weekend had been fantastic. If only things could continue like that.

Mr Tanner tapped his pen on the desk. 'I'd be very sorry to lose you, Suzi. In fact I could see you going far in my little empire. I'm going to be looking for a new head of infants next year and, if things keep going as well as they have been, I hoped you would apply for the position.'

Suzi couldn't believe what he was saying. For Mr Tanner to even think about her being head of infants at this stage in her career was totally unexpected. That clean break she'd been thinking of might still be her best option, but now she had doubts. 'I have to weigh things up,' she said, 'There's a lot to think about. I don't want to dither, but what you've said has made me want to look at this decision again.'

'Good, I'm glad. Even with an excellent reference it may not be too easy finding a job elsewhere which would be a sad loss to the teaching profession. Please, think long and hard about this Suzi. You're a fantastic teacher with a lot to offer. And I want to keep you. Are you going to allow your relationship with a man jeopardise your career? I certainly hope not. You're worth more than that.' Mr Tanner looked at her sternly and she felt like one of the children being reprimanded by him.

14

The telephone ringing through the house in the early hours disturbed Suzi. She was vaguely aware of activity and when she heard Tom's worried voice calling out, she threw back her sheet, pulled on her robe and hurried down the stairs. She didn't want to intrude, but she wanted to help if there was anything she could do.

Cameron was speaking into the telephone in the hall, at the same time reaching out an arm for Tom. But Tom had a troubled look and wouldn't respond to his father. Suzi lifted the boy up swiftly and carried him into the sitting room. She sat on the settee cradling the tearful child and soothingly stroked the damp hair off his forehead. She didn't know what was going on, but she was devastated that Tom was so anxious. When his little body ceased trembling, he cuddled into her. In that moment, she couldn't have loved him more than if he were her own son. The two of them sat with Suzi lovingly rocking him to and fro. When Cameron came into the room, they both jerked with surprise.

Cameron sat on the end of the settee and nodded his thanks to Suzi. 'That was Nana on the phone,' he started to explain, his face ashen with shock. 'Granddad's not feeling well and the doctor wants him to go to the hospital to have some tests tomorrow.' He seemed stumped for words, his mouth opening and closing as he searched for the right ones. 'It's not serious, probably just angina. If that's what it is they can give him some tablets.' He shot Suzi a look as if asking for her input to help reduce Tom's anxiety. Cameron looked in need of comforting words himself, Suzi thought.

'Poor Granddad,' she said. 'It's good that the doctor's looking after him.' She eased Tom over near Cameron and stood up. 'I'm thirsty and I'm going to make some tea for us all.'

Tom was restless and wouldn't stay with Cameron. He followed Suzi out to the kitchen. 'I don't like it when the phone goes in the night,' he confessed.

'It's horrid to be woken up suddenly,' agreed Suzi, filling the kettle. 'Would you get the milk, please?' She knew from her own experience that it was better to be kept busy when something worrying happened.

'It might have been Mummy. When she rings in the night, Dad gets angry sometimes. I want to make her happy, but she doesn't want to talk to me.'

'Grown-ups do silly things occasionally. I'm sure she loves you, Tom.' Suzi couldn't imagine a mother not loving her child. 'I know it's not the same, but I love you.' She put her lips to his hot, red cheek and made a sharp popping sound which made Tom giggle.

Tom seemed slightly more cheerful when they were sitting drinking their tea together. Cameron said, 'I think we should go to Scotland. Nana's going to need a lot of help if Granddad is poorly for a while and needs looking after.'

'Me, you and Suzi, Dad?' He glanced at Suzi. 'You'll like Scotland,' he assured her. 'I hope Nana will have enough beds for us all. Should we ring her and find out, Dad?'

Cameron hesitated. 'Well, Suzi won't be able to go or else Mr Tanner won't have anyone to teach your class. Teachers can't take time off during the term. What I meant was that you and I should go, Tom.'

Without warning Tom banged his cup down on the table and ran up the stairs to his room, slamming the door hard.

'Oh dear,' sighed Cameron. 'What have I done now?'

'Nothing,' replied Suzi. 'He's upset, he doesn't really understand what's going on. He's very fond of your parents and often talks about them. He's worried about his granddad.' She hesitated, unsure if she should pass on what Tom had said. Then, 'Also he thought it was his mother on the phone and that there would be a row.'

Cameron nodded. 'It's happened quite a lot and distressed Tom especially when Wynona won't speak to him. She tends to phone when she's at a party and isn't in the best of moods. She's a difficult and complicated woman. It's strange to think I once had feelings for her.' He took another sip of tea. 'Just so that you know, my father's quite unwell. He's in bed and Mum's going to keep an eye on him tonight. She sounded quite tearful on the phone which isn't like her at all. That's one reason why I think I should go and stay, to take the pressure off Mum. She wouldn't have rung at this time of night if she hadn't been worried. I don't want her to be ill as well.'

Suzi reached for his hand. 'You're doing the right thing.'

'I have to go, Suzi, there's no question of that. I'll leave first thing.'

'Of course you must go. Let's both

settle Tom and try to sleep until it's light, which won't be long. We're all going to be exhausted in the morning.'

Knocking lightly on Tom's door, there was no reply. Cameron edged it open and whispered, 'Can we come in, please?'

There was a sound from the direction of the bed. Cameron looked at Suzi who nodded and gave a small smile of encouragement. Cameron sat on Tom's bed and took his hand, while Suzi hovered near the door, wondering if she was intruding too much between father and son. She didn't want to abandon them, but on the other hand it was a family matter.

'Wouldn't you like to see Nana and Granddad, Tom? You had a great time when we stayed with them. You could go and see the mates you made in Doonston and we could call in at the school if you wanted to. It's just that I feel I have to go. I want to go. They're my mum and dad.'

Tom shuffled down the bed towards

Suzi and clutched at her arm. 'I want to stay here with you. Please. I won't be naughty or anything.'

Pleasure flushed Suzi's cheeks pink, but one look at Cameron told her to be cautious. 'I think you should talk it over with your dad,' she said, trying to lessen the disappointment with a swift kiss on the little boy's head.

'Suzi's got a job, Tom, I told you she's needed at school,' said Cameron. 'We can't expect her to take care of you as well.'

Suzi felt as though she should leave the two of them alone and not interfere. Whatever she thought and felt it was up to them to sort things out between them. She crept out of the room, unsure if they'd even seen her go.

A while later a tap came at Suzi's door. It was Cameron. 'Tom's finally nodded off.' He yawned widely. 'I suppose I should do the same. What I came to say was that Tom says he'd rather stay with you than anything else in the world. He loves Nana and

Granddad, but would like to see them when Granddad's better and they can go fishing. He also said he doesn't want to miss any school. That's great, isn't it? When you think how much he hated it when he first started. I feel awkward asking you, but I don't want to upset him again.'

Suzi grinned. 'I'd love to look after Tom. I can manage, you know, I'm used to children. In fact it will be a pleasure. I'll make sure I keep him busy and he has a lot of fun.'

Cameron gave a tired smile. 'You're wonderful, I can't thank you enough,' he said. 'I should probably go back to bed for a couple of hours, but I don't think I'd be able to sleep.'

'Why don't you stop for a bit and I'll make another hot drink. Make yourself comfortable.' Suzi cleared some papers from the settee before going to the kitchen.

When she returned Cameron was flicking through a magazine which he flung on the coffee table. 'I'm very worried about my dad. It will be a relief to get there and be with him so that I can see for myself how he is.'

'I hope he gets well quickly. Please don't worry about Tom. I promise he'll be fine with me. We've got your mobile number so he can ring you and speak to his nana and granddad. That should reassure him that everything is all right and be a comfort to them, too.'

'Thank you, Suzi. You're so kind and thoughtful. I don't know how I'd manage without you.' Cameron sipped his tea. 'I'm so worked up I can't even decide whether to fly to Scotland or go on the train.'

'I'll see what I can get from the internet. You stay there and relax.'

Having printed off the information she thought would be useful she said, 'Here you are, Cameron.' But he was fast asleep. Fetching a duvet she covered him carefully and lightly kissed his cheek before going to bed.

They were all rather bleary eyed at breakfast, which Suzi had insisted they have at her flat, but she was pleased that Tom seemed fine with the situation.

'I'll still go to Bandit's, won't I?' he asked.

'Everything is going to be exactly the same except when you are at home. Then it will be me looking after you, not your dad. I've been wondering if you want to come and stay in my flat.'

'I like my bedroom. Will you leave your door open at night?'

'If you're happy with that.'

Tom smiled. 'Yeah.' He turned to his father. 'Is it a big aeroplane to Scotland?'

★   ★   ★

'Dad'll be home this evening. He says he's coming to the Sports Day,' called Tom as Suzi made the breakfast toast. Her heart sang as she thought of Cameron's return.

He'd only been away a couple of days, but there had been a gap in her life, even though Tom had been an excellent companion. She'd enjoyed their evenings preparing meals together and playing board games as well as getting Tom to do drawings which he could post to his grandparents in Scotland. They'd both been relieved to hear that Tom's grand-dad was on the mend and he even had a chat with Tom on the phone.

'Granddad feels better now. He wants me to go and stay with them in the holidays so that we can go fishing. Will you come?' Tom asked Suzi.

'We'll see,' was the best she could come up with. 'We'd better decide what we're going to do this evening. Are you coming home with me after school, or going to Dorcas's?'

'Dorcas's,' he replied with no hesitation.

'To see Bandit, I suppose,' said Suzi. She wasn't in the least put out and she admired the honest way in which Tom replied to her questions. It was good that Tom loved Bandit so much and from what she'd witnessed, the feeling was mutual.

Tom poured some juice into his glass. 'And Olivia.' he said.

Suzi hid a smile, but she was curious. 'You get on well with Olivia, don't you? I remember a time when you weren't quite so keen on her.'

'I think I was horrid to her, but I didn't mean to be. Dad said something about not being very nice to people you like.'

'I wonder what he meant by that.'

'It was when Mum had been nasty to me and Dad. Dad said it was because she loved us. But I like being nice best.'

As one, they sniffed the air. 'Burnt toast,' they chorused.

'Again,' offered Tom, chuckling.

Suzi hoped that Cameron would be greeted by a happy, carefree son on his return.

★ ★ ★

'Daddy,' cried Tom as Cameron let himself into the house early that evening. 'We're playing a game. Do you want to have a go?'

'Let me take my luggage upstairs and have a quick shower first, Tommy boy,' said Cameron, 'then we'll play the game. Is that all right? We should phone Nana and Granddad to let them know I'm back home with you. Let me give you a great big hug, I've missed you.'

Suzi felt a bit shy to be in Cameron's part of the house when he returned from Scotland. She knew he would be home that day, but wasn't sure of the precise time. He looked tired, pale and drained.

True to his word, when Cameron came downstairs newly showered and in a fresh pair of trousers and a t-shirt, he got Tom to press the numbers on the phone. Listening to them conversing happily, Suzi silently left them to it and went upstairs to her flat.

She'd miss her evenings with Tom, but she had a lot of work to do as the term's end approached. Writing report summaries for all the children in her class took time and concentration. Also the Sports Day would soon be upon them. The school year was whizzing by and she still had to decide about giving in her notice to Mr Tanner. Along with that was the dreadful thought of how she would break the news to Cameron and Tom that she would be leaving not only the flat, but also the area.

★   ★   ★

During the sports Suzi was aware that Fred had brought Dorcas and that Cameron was on the sidelines cheering on the children, but she had no time to stop and chat. By the end of the afternoon she was exhausted and, after seeing all the over-excited children off with their parents and various other proud relatives, she longed to go home and relax. As she walked up the stairs she could see Cameron was outside her flat.

'Caught me!'

'What are you up to?' She had to laugh at his surprised expression.

'I was just leaving these outside your door. I didn't want to disturb you when you got back.' He produced a huge bunch of summer flowers from behind his back. 'Didn't grow them myself, of course.'

'They're beautiful. What are they for?'

'You.'

'But why? It's not my birthday.'

'Because I want to say sorry for all the hassle you've had to endure since living here. I'm sorry for everything. I thought it would be good for you to live with us, but there's been one thing after another. Also as a thankyou for looking after Tom for me and keeping him happy.' He held the flowers out to her. 'Not much in way of recompense, but I do have some other ideas.'

'They're beautiful.' She breathed in their heady smell. 'Thank you, Cameron. Actually I have something I'd like to talk to you about. Will you come in?' She hadn't planned on telling Cameron her plans now, but somehow this

293

seemed as good a time as any.

'I'll arrange the flowers if you give me a vase. Tom is round at Dorcas's again. It's difficult to prise him away.'

'Do you think this vase is big enough? Shall I fill it with water?' Suzi asked as she watched Cameron busy himself with the flower food. 'You should be very proud of Tom. He's a lovely boy and he's been through a lot. You're a great dad.'

'I *am* proud of him, but I'm not proud of myself. I've made so many mistakes. I should have finished with Wynona a long time ago. She's caused us both nothing but distress. I haven't loved her for a very long time. And since I realised I was finally through with her I've been protecting Tom from yet more possible heartache.' He looked across at her.

'The flowers are beautiful, thank you. It was kind of you to bring them.' She tried to keep her voice even. 'I understand completely about protecting Tom because you're bound to put him first. You have to.'

Cameron nodded in agreement and Suzi felt as though her heart was in pieces. She took a deep breath. 'I invited you in because I have something important I'd like to talk to you about.' Suzi wasn't sure if she was making the right decision, but maybe a fresh start might be just what she needed. However, she wanted to discuss things with someone whose opinion she could trust. 'I've spoken to Mr Tanner about leaving London at Christmas.'

Suzi had just wanted to talk over the arguments for and against her leaving, but Cameron had merely thrown the rubbish in the bin and muttered that he wouldn't be holding her back. Then he'd slammed out of the flat.

★　★　★

Cameron came down to his part of the house bewildered and deeply unhappy. He thought he'd got it right with the flowers and he'd desperately hoped that

Suzi would accept an invitation to an evening out with him — just him. Sometimes he couldn't understand Suzi. Whenever they'd spent time together he'd been so enchanted with her company and from her laughter and actions, he was sure she enjoyed being with him. Hadn't she said so, even when things got a bit awkward? He remembered the meal in the restaurant, their visit to the park, their gallery outing and the picnic. He thought they were getting close and then she found an excuse to distance herself from him. He was sure she wasn't playing games like Wynona used to do, but there was still a wave of bitterness inside him. He should never have said they could only be friends.

He couldn't bear to put either Tom or himself through more of the heartache they'd endured, but he'd thought that maybe with Suzi things could be different. He'd even toyed with the idea of what a wonderful mother figure she would make if she *consented to share his and Tom's lives. Why was she leaving? He was sure she was happy with the flat and everyone at the school seemed to admire her. There was no doubt she was a good teacher. He mustn't hold her back. Perhaps it was a promotion she was getting. Not being able to bear being under the same roof as Suzi at the moment, Cameron slammed out of the house without an idea of where he was going or what he was going to do.*

★ ★ ★

Suzi gazed at the flowers through teetering tears. They were so pretty and delicate and Cameron had chosen her favourite sunshine colours. She still wasn't sure what they were in aid of. When he'd first given them to her she'd held a shred of hope that he was going to ask her out, especially when he mentioned Wynona again and the fact that he no longer loved her. But there was Tom. It always came back to Tom, quite rightly. She didn't know why Cameron hadn't been able to stay and help her make her decision. She'd wanted his advice and he'd let her down.

Feeling stifled in the flat and having heard Cameron leave his part of the house, Suzi decided to go into the garden. The hard, dry earth felt warm beneath her bare feet and the dried out grass tickled her toes. Looking around the garden, she realised it had been neglected over the past few weeks. Often Cameron, with Tom's help, had pulled out weeds and kept the grass short. But even taking the scorching sun into consideration, the garden was depressing now with no one playing in it. Briefly, Suzi compared it with Dorcas's overgrown area at the back of her house; that had a vibrancy which couldn't be measured up with this. It was as if it mirrored her own misery. As sadness settled over her again, she hurried into the shed, dragged out some tools and started hacking away at the straggling edges of the lawn and flower beds.

Having put her energy into the task, she sat back on her heels and admired what she'd done. It wasn't great, but it was a lot better. Her mind felt calmed also. She stretched herself out on her back and closed her eyes. Something that Dorcas had said in the hospital came to her: if Matt and she exchanged roles she would want him to be happy. Of course she would. Then she thought of Cameron; she *did* love him and she wanted him to be happy too — but he wasn't, he looked to be just as miserable as she was. Perhaps they did both want the same thing. Which was to be with each other and not to cause Tom any pain.

Going over to the guinea pig run, she smiled down at them. Even on this scorching day they were huddled together in a corner. As she watched them, they moved slightly, shifting this way and that almost, it seemed, as if

299

they were trying to shield each other from the sun even though the shade of a tree protected them. Their tiny whiskers quivered and they emitted little squeaks as if they were chatting to each other.

Suzi eased a finger through the wire netting. 'Hi there, you two. You sound happy.' They replied by mumbling at her again and snuggling up tighter to each other. Then Suzi understood what it was. Pinky and Porky were happy just to be together. They needed each other. That was how she felt about Cameron; when he wasn't around she was miserable.

Suzi scrambled to her feet and rushed up to her flat to change her sweaty, grubby clothes. After a cooling shower, she quickly chose a silk dress of cream with blue mixed splash which showed off her lightly tanned skin. To match the ribbon detailing, she decided on a pair of blue strappy stilettos. Feeling flirty and feminine, she went downstairs and waited in Cameron's sitting room until he returned. Idly she sifted through his music collection, selected a CD and put it on. She heard the key in the front door and held her breath.

15

When Cameron heard music coming from his part of the house, his first thought was how wonderful it would be if Suzi had come to look for him, to tell him she wasn't leaving after all and that everything would be all right. But that sort of fairytale ending would only be for story books. He was in the real world and old enough to know better. He entered his sitting room and there she was, looking beautiful and radiant. She glided towards him. Before she could speak, Cameron took her in his arms and danced her around the tiny space.

'Let's dance, not talk,' he said, his voice husky.

★   ★   ★

Suzi was aware of his strong arms around her, and her hammering heart.

When the music finished, neither of them pulled apart. She whispered, 'I can't be content with anything less than true love.' Cameron turned his head and looked down at her, waiting silently. 'I don't think I ever loved Matt in the way that I love you.' It was something she'd constantly asked herself over and over during the time she'd been getting to know Cameron. Hers and Matt's love had been idyllic at the time and they had truly been in love. But it was as if she'd been a different person then. Of course she'd been a girl when she'd first loved Matt and she'd never questioned the reality of that love. Now she was a woman and she loved Cameron with a fierce passion, of that she had no doubt.

Cameron drew her even closer to him, his lips on hers.

It was Suzi who made the first move to part. 'I love you, Cameron,' she explained hesitantly, 'but there's a lot to be considered regarding Tom. I don't want to spoil your relationship and he's got to get used to the fact that Wynona won't be around him much. It's a lot for a young child to take on board. We must both be sure that Tom is happy. He needs stability and your care and love more than ever.'

'I love you too, Suzi. Thank you for being so understanding about Tom. When I returned from Scotland it was obvious to me that he'd enjoyed his time with you looking after him. He couldn't stop talking about all the things you did together. He even mentioned you before telling me about Bandit. I do understand that it's a lot to ask you to take not only me, but also my son, permanently into your life. You have to be sure that you want that commitment, just as I have to be sure that Tom will be happy. These things take time, but I think we're nearly there, don't you? But please put my mind at rest now and say that you won't be leaving.'

Suzi put her arms around him and

kissed him. 'I never want to leave you, Cameron.'

★ ★ ★

Suzi hummed as she mixed flour, sugar and butter together, squinting at the recipe book from time to time. Ahead of her was the last week of the term, but first there was the school fete this weekend. Carried along with the enthusiasm of the rest of the staff and children, she'd agreed to make fairy cakes, flapjack and a chocolate gateau. She found the task calming and looked forward to seeing the rows of goodies laid out on the worktop.

With the tins in the oven, she set the timer and put the utensils in warm soapy water to soak. Then she settled down with a crime novel she'd been meaning to read for a long while.

The cakes were taking forever; they must be done by now. As she opened the kitchen door, she smelt the burning immediately. What had gone wrong?

Black smoke wafted out from the oven. The fairy cakes looked as if they'd had an evil spell cast over them, the flapjack was charred and the chocolate cake didn't look at all appetising. Realising that she must have set the timer for far too long, she scraped the burnt offerings into a bag to take out to the rubbish bin at the back of the house.

'Suzi.'

She leaned against the wall of the house when she heard Cameron calling.

'We haven't seen you all morning. We're just off to the park, would you like to come with us?'

'What's that funny smell?' asked Tom, wriggling his nose.

Suzi smiled weakly. 'I've been baking some cakes for the fete, but they didn't go too well. All black and horrible, I'm afraid. They're going in the dustbin.' She opened the bag for them to see, expecting them to make fun of her.

'Oh dear,' said Cameron. 'What a shame. I bet it took ages to cook those.'

'I set the timer wrongly and then I

got caught up with my book. A really gripping whodunit.' Suzi tried to make a joke out of it, but she wasn't feeling amused at all.

'Do you want me to help you make some more?' asked Tom.

What a sweet little boy he was. Suzi looked up at Cameron and saw him gazing at her longingly. She gave him a wide smile before replying to Tom. 'Thanks, but you go and enjoy the park with your dad. It's better to be out in the sunshine than in a hot kitchen.'

Suzi went back to the flat and started her baking all over again, deciding to stay in there until she could turn out a respectable batch of things to sell. She'd just make flapjack this time as she'd run out of eggs.

* * *

In the morning, Suzi was awake early and ready to leave, looking forward to the day ahead and hoping she wouldn't disturb Cameron or Tom. As she passed through the hall downstairs she saw a foil-covered tray with a note on the top. It was addressed to her:

Tom and I made these for you to take to the fete. We hope they're all right for the cake stall.

Slowly, Suzi lifted the cover and there were thirty-six butterfly cakes sitting pertly in little rainbow cases. Tears threatened as she lifted the tray to carry it out to her car. What a wonderful gesture. She imagined them both in their kitchen striving to produce these just for her. What a brilliant pair they were. Having stowed the cakes carefully on the back seat, Suzi buckled herself in and drove off quickly as the threatened tears started to flow. Time and again Cameron had shown his love for her, not merely told her in words. How she loved that man; she wasn't prepared to wait for him any longer. She'd tell him as soon as she saw him.

★ ★ ★

The school fete attracted a lot of people, not just parents and relatives of the children, but local people from all over the area.

'I'm glad you changed your mind about leaving, Suzi,' beamed Mr Tanner approaching the stall.

'So am I, Mr Tanner,' she replied. 'Thank you for the advice you gave me. You're a very kind man.'

Mr Tanner blushed and cleared his throat. Then he said, 'Those cakes look delicious, I think I'll buy a couple to have with a cup of tea.' He handed over the money to Tom who was helping out at the stall.

'Does he need any change?' whispered Olivia to Tom as he confidently took the money. Suzi watched as the two children counted together, adding up the cost of the two cakes. They were the best of friends now and wouldn't let anyone say a bad word against the other. Just like she'd been with Matt. Suzi was pleased she could say that now, if only to herself, without the usual black misery descending upon her.

'Come on, Fred, get your money out. I'm going to have some of those.' Dorcas was back to her usual cheery self.

'As far as I'm concerned you can have the lot,' said Fred, taking his arm from around her to find some cash.

'Fred and me will take over from you, Suzi. You have a look around.' She spoke to Tom and Olivia. 'Will you two help us?'

'You eat your cakes, Dorcas. We can take the money,' Tom assured her.

Dorcas bit into a butterfly cake and licked the crumbs and cream from her lips. Then she said to Suzi, 'The fete's going very well this year. I think you getting the parents involved with the play helped. Quite a few of them said they feel more a part of the school now than they did before and they've volunteered for loads of things this afternoon.'

As Dorcas organised everyone, Suzi

laughed and wandered round greeting parents and locals she'd got to know during her time at the school. Up ahead of her a huge queue had formed. What was going on? Inquisitively she went to have a look.

Sitting bolt upright in the stocks was Cameron, his rumble of laughter clearly identifying him to Suzi. Children and adults alike were hurling wet sponges at him. The pupils egged Suzi on, 'Why don't you have a go, Miss. If you hit him you get a free turn.'

'Okay, then, I will,' agreed Suzi. She took careful aim and then half-heartedly tossed the sponge at Cameron not minding if she hit or missed him. As the sponge caught his handsome face squarely and water trickled down his shirt, Suzi was propelled towards him by an unknown force. And there she was holding his hands, her lips on his. 'I love you, Cameron,' she burst out. Her cheek on his, she whispered into his ear, 'I'm ready to spend the rest

311

of my life with you.'

'There's nothing I want more,' replied Cameron. 'I love you, too, Suzi.' They were immune to the rest of the world, to the whoops from their audience and anything other than the two of them.

Behind them, Dorcas laughed as she picked up a soaking sponge and threw it at the loving couple. 'It took you long enough,' she yelled. Then she took out a little wooden sign and placed it by the stocks. 'Closed.'

THE END

Other titles in the
Linford Romance Library:

ROMANCE IN THE AIR

Pat Posner

After ending a relationship she discovered was based on lies, Annie Layton has sworn off men. When her employers, Edmunds' Airways, tell her they're expanding, she eagerly agrees to help set up the sister company. Moving up north will get her away from her ex — and the Air Ministry official who's been playing havoc with her emotions. But Annie hadn't known exactly who she'd be working with ... Will she find herself pitched headlong into further heartache?